"Alex, they're coming. We have to hurry."

Alex looped the rope around the tree and started tying it off. Before he'd finished, he heard voices coming from just over the ridge. He took Rachel's hand and they headed to the edge of the creek.

"You should go ahead of me. I'm positive it will hold your weight. I'm not sure about mine. If they reach me before I can cross, cut the rope and get out of here. Find Liam."

He didn't get to finish before she shook her head. "I'm not leaving you behind, Alex. We're in this together."

His gaze clung to hers. So many unspoken feelings weighed on his mind. He had to protect her.

"Rachel, I..." He wasn't sure what he wanted to tell her, only that he needed her to understand that he still cared about her.

She placed her finger over his lips. "No, you're going to make it and I'm not leaving this area without you. We're going to find Liam together, and this is all going to be a bad memory someday."

Mary Alford was inspired to become a writer after reading romantic suspense greats Victoria Holt and Phyllis A. Whitney. Soon, creating characters and throwing them into dangerous situations that test their faith came naturally for Mary. In 2012 Mary entered the Speed Dating contest hosted by Love Inspired Suspense and later received "the call." Writing for Love Inspired Suspense has been a dream come true for Mary.

Books by Mary Alford

Love Inspired Suspense

Forgotten Past
Rocky Mountain Pursuit
Deadly Memories
Framed for Murder
Standoff at Midnight Mountain

STANDOFF AT MIDNIGHT MOUNTAIN

MARY ALFORD

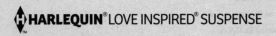

HARLEQUIN® LOVE INSPIRED® SUSPENSE

Recycling programs
for this product may
not exist in your area.

LOVE INSPIRED BOOKS

ISBN-13: 978-1-335-54389-9

Standoff at Midnight Mountain

Copyright © 2018 by Mary Eason

www.Harlequin.com

Printed in U.S.A.

Yea, though I walk through the valley of the shadow of death, I will fear no evil: for thou art with me; thy rod and thy staff they comfort me.
—*Psalms* 23:4

To first loves.

ONE

The still of the peaceful Wyoming morning was broken by the noise of a vehicle approaching. Rachel Simmons breathed a heartfelt sigh of relief. Alex was here. Maybe now, with his help, she could finally get some answers into her brother's mysterious disappearance.

Outside, the car came to a stop. A door slammed, followed by footsteps, then someone knocked noisily on her door, jarring her spent nerves.

She hurried to answer it. With her hand resting on the door handle, a voice she didn't recognize spoke, stopping her in her tracks. "Ma'am, I'm sorry to trouble you so early, but my wife and I seem to have lost our way." A pause followed, almost as if the man was waiting for her response, yet she couldn't manage a word. Who was this person? "Can you tell me how to get back to the highway?"

Close by, her faithful golden retriever, Callie,

growled low, the hackles along the ridge of her back standing at full attention. Callie charged for the door, sniffing and barking her alarm. A chill sped down Rachel's spine, her internal radar skyrocketed. She'd been living on edge since her brother's last visit. Now, after trying to reach Liam for more than a week without avail, she couldn't shake the feeling that something bad had happened. It was the reason why she'd called in her CIA colleague, Alex Booth.

"Quiet, Callie," Rachel whispered close to the dog's ear. Callie stopped her barking and sat back on her haunches, but the ridge didn't go away.

Nothing but the tiniest rays of light from the woodstove in the great room would be visible through the curtained windows. It was four in the morning. How had this man ended up at her door so early, and why would he believe anyone in the house was awake at such an hour?

What he'd said finally registered through her troubled thoughts and she shivered. *Ma'am*. He knew she was here alone.

Rachel grabbed her constant companion as of late, the one piece from her past life as a CIA agent she still possessed: her Glock.

Her place was in the middle of forty heavily wooded acres and not even close to a main highway. No one would just happen by here, especially at this hour. She clutched the Glock tighter. The man's sudden appearance smelled of some type of setup.

"I realize it's early, ma'am, but we really need some directions and my cell phone has died." His tone had taken a turn toward sharp. He was growing impatient with her. "Can my wife and I come in and warm up for a bit and maybe use your phone?"

Rachel ticked off every tense beat of her heart while she tried to decide what to do next. Where was Alex? She had expected him some time ago. Did this man's sudden appearance have anything to do with Alex's delay? She didn't want to think about her call being responsible for harm coming to Alex.

One of the front porch boards squeaked as the man shifted his weight. He wasn't leaving and she had a choice to make. She needed to get rid of him before trying Alex's cell phone. If this man was up to no good, she could be putting Alex's life in danger. That is, if she hadn't already…

Don't let me make the wrong decision…

Rachel hurried to the window closest to the door and inched the curtains apart. A tall, bulky man dressed in dark clothing, a knit cap pulled over most of the top of his head, stood on her porch.

Callie followed her, growling like crazy. She was picking up on her owner's unease.

Rachel's gaze slid to the car parked out front. A woman was seated inside, watching the man. Was she his wife as the man had said, or was there something more going on here? "I'm sorry, but I don't have a phone," she called out in answer to his request to borrow hers. "But if you go back the way you came, you'll run into the main highway without a problem."

The man took a step closer to the door.

"It's awfully cold out, ma'am. If we could come inside just for a minute?" He attempted a smile that didn't come close to reaching his steely eyes.

Rachel spotted a bulge beneath the man's jacket. He was armed! Out of the corner of her eye, she noticed that the woman had opened the car door and was getting out, her hand tucked inside her jacket. Why would two innocent travelers need to be armed?

"How did you know I lived here alone?" Rachel immediately regretted the question. She'd given away too much.

"Must have seen it on your mailbox," he muttered, not even trying to hide the lie. The only name on the mailbox was Simmons, the alias Rachel had taken when she'd left the life of a spy behind and returned to Midnight Mountain.

Fear settled into the pit of her stomach when the man whipped his gun from its holster. Callie forgot her command of silence and began barking ferociously. The truth became apparent. These two hadn't just happened by here. They were here deliberately…for her.

Rachel hurried for the door, making sure all the locks were securely in place. Seconds later, the man opened fire, bullets riddling her door.

Rachel automatically hit the floor. Keeping as much out of the line of fire as she possibly could, she crawled on her hands and knees until she reached the kitchen, with Callie close by, growling and shaking with fear.

Behind her, she could hear the man yelling to the woman to cover him while he leveraged his full weight against the locked door, sending it rattling on its hinges.

After her brother's strange behavior before he had left to meet with his asset more than a week ago and had seemingly dropped off the face of the earth, Rachel was positive that these two intruders were somehow connected to Liam's disappearance. If she stayed here, she'd be dead before Alex could reach her. She prayed that he was safe and had just been delayed.

If she was going to live, she had to get away now. Her frantic brain tried to come up with an exit strategy, but there was really only one way out.

Once she reached the kitchen, she grabbed her coat from where she kept it close to the back door. Keeping as low as she could, she ran out the door with Callie at her heels, before her only means of escape evaporated. What if there were more men surrounding the house? She could be walking into a trap. Holding on to what was left of her courage, she raced for the woods off to the right.

Once she reached the trees close to the house, Rachel heard the man finally break through her front door. They'd breached the house. It wouldn't take them long to realize she'd gone out the back.

"Hurry, Callie," she urged the dog as they forged deeper into the woods.

"There's no sign of *them* inside. I'm guessing they were never here." The man's voice carried through the still predawn. "They're both still up on the mountain somewhere. We know one or both are injured. Find her. We need to put a lid on this. Now. Too much is at stake and we don't know if Carlson told anyone else."

Reality shot through Rachel like a lightning bolt. He was talking about Liam. If what the man said were true, her brother was hurt…or worse. More than ever, she knew she had to find

Liam, which meant she'd need to get out of here alive and before they could capture her.

Callie let out a tense-sounding growl as they continued frantically running through the dense wooded area. Low-slung branches tangled in Rachel's hair and snagged her face, making it impossible to make much progress. Every step she made jarring. The cold of the early morning chilling her to the bone.

The dog was on edge just as she was. Callie had faced down lots of predators, bears included, but she'd never been involved in a gunfight.

Rachel stopped long enough to gain her bearings. From where she stood, she could just see the back of the house through the trees. Two people emerged from inside, flashlights shining all around. She ducked when the light hit close.

"Over there," the man yelled, homing in on the area where she stood with his flashlight beam.

Rachel turned on her heel and started running again, her heart thundering in her chest with each step. She'd been out of the game for a long time. She wasn't used to being hunted.

Callie soon took the lead. They'd barely managed a handful of steps when a round of shots whistled past Rachel's head. Close enough for her to feel the breeze it kicked up.

She tucked closer to the ground, almost doubled over, and ran.

"Hurry—she's getting away." The woman spoke for the first time. Rachel didn't recognize her voice either, but she detected a faint accent that she couldn't place. Who were these people and how were they connected to Liam?

Some distance behind her, the rustling of brush assured her that her pursuers had now entered the woods. Callie growled at the noise and turned back in a defensive stance, ready to charge the enemy. The dog was overly protective of Rachel, but she couldn't let her companion get caught in the line of fire.

"Come, Callie. Hurry," Rachel ordered, and the dog reluctantly abandoned her defense and followed Rachel.

Where was Alex? He should have been here by now. Had something happened to him? Fear shot through her body.

With her thoughts churning in a dozen different directions, Rachel tried to come up with a means of escape on foot. She had the advantage. She knew the area like the back of her hand. If she could make it to her neighbor's house, she could call for help from there. But if Liam's suspicions were true? What then? Liam was a seasoned CIA agent. If what he believed proved real, then she could be walking straight into the enemy's arms by calling in the authorities.

Rachel didn't dare take a direct path to the Reagans' place. It wouldn't be long before her pursuers figured out the direction she'd gone. She'd be bringing her troubles to the Reagans' doorstep. She couldn't do that.

"This way," the woman yelled. "I see her up ahead." More shots rang out; bullets flew past, one barely missing her shoulder. They were gaining! Would Tom Reagan hear the shots and come to investigate?

Please, God, no.

She had a feeling these people wouldn't be opposed to killing anyone who got in their way. Even someone as innocent as Tom.

Rachel shoved branches out of her way as she ran blindly through the woods. Just in front of her, Callie suddenly stopped dead in her tracks. Rachel almost tripped over the dog in the process. There was just time to sidestep in an attempt to avoid the mishap when she slammed headfirst into something warm and solid. A man! He reached out and grabbed her tight. One thought raced through her head. They'd found her. She had to get away if she wanted to live.

Panicked, Rachel fought with everything she had, but she was no match for the man's strength.

Before she could scream, a hand clasped over her mouth and the man pulled her close.

"Don't scream, Rachel. It's me." *Alex!* He was alive and he was here.

Relief made her knees weak. She hugged him close and struggled to let go of the panic still electrifying her nervous system.

"I heard the shots from the road and guessed something had gone wrong. We need to get out of here fast. Those shots sounded close. And this place is crawling with men. My car's just over there." He pointed up ahead, then glanced in the direction Rachel had come. "They're almost here. Run for the car. I'll try to distract them. I'll be right behind you," he added when she didn't budge.

Alex gave her a gentle shove in that direction, but Rachel stood her ground. She might not be part of the CIA anymore, but one thing was still ingrained in her brain: you never left your partner behind.

Alex drew his Glock and opened fire. Rachel didn't hesitate before doing the same.

A scream of pain rang out. They'd hit one of their pursuers. Rachel didn't believe it would slow the other down one little bit.

She turned and hurried toward the car with Callie. Alex cleared the woods shortly after her and the dog.

Before they could reach the vehicle, someone opened fire on them. Rachel ducked for cover behind the side of the car. She caught a glimpse of a man holding his shoulder. He was injured but it didn't stop him from shooting at them. Alex managed to get off several rounds, forcing the man to hide behind a nearby tree to avoid another direct hit. Where was the woman?

"Hurry, Rachel," Alex yelled as he opened the driver's-side door and lunged inside. Rachel yanked her door open. Callie hit the front seat first. She followed seconds later.

"Go, go, go," she urged in an unsteady voice, reflecting the magnitude of what had just happened.

Alex put the vehicle in Drive and floored it while staying as low as he possibly could and still see where he was going.

Rachel glanced behind them. The man had stepped from his tree coverage and began shooting at them again. Several other men joined him, all firing. The back window shattered. Rachel tucked down low while from the back seat Callie let out a frightened yelp.

"It's okay, girl. Everything is going to be okay." She stroked the dog's fur, trying to reassure them both.

Alex jerked the wheel to the right to avoid another hit. The car veered close to the edge of the road. He quickly corrected and managed to keep them from crashing just in time.

Soon, at least four sets of headlights flashed behind them. The men were coming full force. Alex floored the gas pedal once more in an attempt to lose them.

"What happened back there?" he asked, the tension in his voice evident. He spared her a glance as he continued to push the car to its limit, still unable to shake the vehicles.

Numb from shock, Rachel shook her head. "I don't know." It was the truth, but she could see that he didn't believe it. Not that she could blame him. People just didn't come to your house and start shooting at you for no reason. "A man and a woman showed up at my door. He said they were lost. I could tell he was armed. When I refused to let him come inside, the man started shooting at me. Alex, I barely got away…" She stopped for a much-needed breath and glanced down at her hands. They were shaking. She'd almost died. Both of them had come close.

"There's no way they just happened to show up at my front door. This is connected to Liam's disappearance somehow. What I don't understand is how they knew where to find me?" Rachel had gone to great lengths to disguise her identity after leaving the Agency. She'd created an alias last name. Even after she'd gotten married, she hadn't taken her husband's name simply because there was always the chance that her past might come looking for her. No one would be able to track her by that association.

Rachel cast a suspicious look Alex's way. "Did you tell anyone you were coming here?"

His response came quick, his tone reflecting his hurt. "Of course not. Rach, you asked me not to tell anyone, so I didn't. But the woods were crawling with people back there. I'm surprised they didn't spot me before I was able to reach you. Or hear my car, for that matter." He shook his head. "You said on the phone you hadn't spoken to Liam in more than a week. You believe he's gone missing?" She nodded. She hadn't said as much when she'd called, but Alex had guessed. "Why do you think that? How does this ambush fit into Liam's disappearance?"

She'd been brief on the phone. Afraid to tell him her worst fears. "I don't know how this fits into it, but I know Liam, and I *haven't* heard from him in over a week." She realized how foolish she sounded right now, but she knew if her brother were able to, he would have been in touch by now.

Rachel kept a nervous eye on the vehicles behind them. So far, Alex had been able to keep them at a distance, but they had to find a way to lose them soon if they were going to help Liam.

"We need to get off this road, Alex. It'll drop us into the town of Midnight Mountain, and who knows how many more men they have waiting for us there." She pointed up ahead. "There's a side road coming up on the right, just after we make this next curve around the mountain. Take it."

Alex nodded and turned his full attention on his driving. When the road in question came into sight, he slowed the car's speed slightly.

"Hang on," he warned. Alex was an excellent driver and yet it took all his skills to make the curve at the high rate of speed. Once they'd safely exited, he killed the lights to give them a fighting chance.

With adrenaline pumping through her body like crazy, Rachel spotted the vehicles swerving onto the same road. "They're still coming." She racked her brain to recall the layout of this less-traveled road. It had just recently opened after being closed for the winter. Even though it was late March and springtime in other parts of the country, here in the mountains snow still hung around, especially in the high places.

"Hold on. There's another less-traveled side road just past this next bend. It's pretty obscured from view. Unless you know it's there you probably won't see it. If we can make that, with the lights out, I think we have a chance of getting away undetected."

Alex slowed just enough to make the turn, then gassed on the accelerator once more. So far, none of the cars appeared to be following.

He glanced in the rearview mirror and then at her. She could tell he believed she knew more than what she'd told him so far and he was waiting for her to talk. Did she dare voice her concerns aloud?

With everything that happened, especially after what Liam had told her, she didn't know who to trust. But this was Alex. He'd dropped everything to come to her aid simply because she'd asked for help.

"Rachel, please tell me what's going on," he asked quietly.

If what she suspected were true, had she put Alex's career, if not his life, in danger by asking for his help? In spite of everything they'd been through in the past, she still cared for him. They'd grown up here in these mountains, the three of them. She still considered Alex a friend.

"Look, these guys have proven they aren't about to give up until they get what they're after. You called me in because you needed my help. You can trust me, Rachel. Let me help you."

As she looked into his eyes, she knew, no

matter what, Alex would never betray her or Liam. She *could* trust him.

She blew out a breath and shook her head. If it were anyone else, Alex might have thought she was overreacting. But she was former CIA herself. He knew she wasn't imagining things. That was why he'd come so quickly.

"Liam told me he was scheduled to meet with his asset after he left my place, but I could see he was anxious about something. I'd never seen him look so worried before. He kept checking out the window as if he were expecting someone to show up." She stopped for a breath, then told Alex what Liam had said about the newest terror threat he'd been chasing. Liam didn't say how, but he believed the person he was after might be closer than Liam had originally believed. At the time, Rachel hadn't been sure what to make of Liam's comments.

She couldn't read Alex's opinion of this. "Yesterday, I was putting away some clothes and I found Liam's phone along with a map that he'd left in my bedroom dresser drawer. The phone was turned off. He'd wanted me to find them after he left. There was a location pinpointed on the map along with an initial and a phone number on the back..." She stopped and realized how little it was to go on. Liam had been trying to tell her something. His warning had been chilling. If only she knew what he was trying to say!

"Did you call the number?" Alex asked, and she nodded.

"Although it took me several hours to work up the nerve." He smiled at this and clasped her hand for a second.

"I didn't recognize the voice on the other end. A few hours later, those people showed up at my door. It's no coincidence." She shuddered at the thought.

Rachel didn't understand what was going on, but the couple that came to her house knew about her brother. They'd known Liam had been up on the mountain along with someone else, presumably his asset. They believed he was injured and possibly still there. Would she and Alex be too late? Would they find her brother dead? She couldn't bear the thought.

Lack of sleep made it hard to keep her thoughts focused, but she had to try. Liam needed her.

"Did Liam ever mention knowing someone whose name starts with the initial *D*? A friend maybe?"

She watched as Alex tried to recollect any such name. He shook his head. "No, never. But one thing's clear. Liam would never have left those things behind if he wasn't worried about something. He wanted you to have them in case…"

He left the rest unsaid but she knew what he meant. In case Liam didn't make it down from the mountain.

"Did you check Liam's phone for calls? Maybe someone he called can help us figure out where he's at?"

She had checked, and the results were disappointing. "I did. It was as if he'd deliberately cleared out all the numbers."

Rachel could tell this didn't sit well with Alex, yet he tried to reassure her. "Maybe he was afraid the phone might fall into the wrong hands. He could have been expecting those people to show up at your place."

None of these options helped ease her fears any, and he must have seen it.

"First things first. We need to get out of sight as quickly as possible. Once we have a chance to breathe, we can come up with a plan to locate Liam." Alex smiled and then turned his attention to the road ahead while uneasy thoughts churned through Rachel's mind.

Who was this new player Liam had uncovered and how were they connected to her brother's vanishing? There had to be more to the story than what Rachel knew, because right now, all she had to go on were bits and pieces of a puzzle that might well lead them to a deadly conclusion. And every minute they didn't know the answer, Liam's life was in danger.

Alex was still shell-shocked by the things that had happened since he'd returned to his hometown of Midnight Mountain; his head burst with unanswered questions. His fear for Liam's safety wasn't eased one little bit by what Rachel had told him.

While they might have lost the men chasing them for now, they weren't out of the woods yet. Without knowing why those men were coming after Rachel and Liam so mercilessly, he had no idea what they were up against. There could be more armed men saturating the surrounding countryside and staked out in town waiting to ambush them.

Alex made several more evasive turns as a precaution before they shot out onto the outskirts of town in the opposite direction from the house where Rachel was living.

A quick glance in the rearview mirror assured him they weren't being followed—yet.

He slowed the car's speed and glanced over at Rachel. "They'll be looking for this car. It's not safe to be out in the open like this for long."

Alex tried to recall some of the back roads they'd once used as shortcuts when they were younger, but he'd been gone from the area since his parents passed away in a car wreck his senior year. He'd graduated high school and went away to college. After that, he'd joined the CIA and his work had taken him around the world. He hadn't been home since.

Rachel pointed up ahead. "There's a county road a little ways from here. And I know where we can hide out for a while. Maybe they'll think we've left the area and they'll move on if they can't find us right away."

Alex turned onto a less-maintained road filled with potholes. As much as he wanted to believe it, these men had proven themselves ruthless.

"At least we've lost them for now." He sounded much calmer than he felt inside. In the space of a less than eight hours, his life had been turned upside down. His friend was missing, and he and Rachel were working together again to try to figure out what had happened.

There was little doubt in his mind that Rachel's worry for Liam's safety was valid. She wasn't the type to jump at shadows.

"Those people were there because of Liam. They thought he'd be at my house." She turned in her seat so that she could look Alex in the eye. "He's in serious trouble. He's up there on Midnight Mountain somewhere…and I'm not sure if he's still alive."

What she said struck like a blow to the gut. "You think Liam may already be dead?" Alex couldn't allow himself to even contemplate the possibility. He and Liam were closer than friends. They'd grown up together. They were like brothers.

"I don't know." She shook her head, her tone conveying her fear for her brother.

In spite of what had happened today, one thing bothered Alex a lot. Why was Rachel so convinced that Liam was in trouble with very little to back up the conviction? Was he missing something, or was there more to the story than what she'd told him so far?

"How do you know for certain that Liam's not still on a mission? You must have something more to go on than the fact that you haven't spoken to him in a while and he left his phone and a map at your place. I know the two of you are close, but you realize it's not uncommon for an agent to go dark for a long time when he or she is working a lead."

He barely got the words out before she rejected his theory. "It's more than that, Alex, and I know it." Her words wiped away what little bit of hope he still held on to. His heart wouldn't let him go there. He couldn't imagine losing Liam.

"Have you spoken to his handler?" He sure hoped she'd overlooked something. While Alex knew the information the CIA would give out to a civilian was limited, she was different. She'd once been one of them.

"I've tried. Seth isn't answering. And when I called his boss, he gave me the company line. He said he couldn't discuss any details concerning Liam's mission. When I told him I was worried Liam might be in trouble, he pretty much dismissed me. He told me that I, of all people, should know that when an agent is on a mission, they go radio silent."

Alex felt his hands were tied as to what to do next. "I need to reach out to Liam's boss right away. Perhaps he'll talk to me."

He barely finished the sentence. "No, you can't."

Alex stared at her, his eyes wide with surprise. "Why not?"

Rachel turned away in a defensive manner. There was something she didn't want him to know. "You just can't, okay."

She didn't fully trust him yet and that hurt like crazy. Was it because of what happened between them, or who he worked for?

He blew out a frustrated sigh and agreed to go along with what she wanted for the time being. "All right, I won't make that call just yet."

It would be up to him and Rachel to put the pieces together and bring Liam home alive.

Alex glanced in the back seat where the dog had finally settled down, although she still kept a close eye on Alex. It was clear the dog was protective of Rachel.

"Who's your friend?" He nodded behind them when she looked at him in confusion.

"Oh. Her name is Callie, and she's been my good friend for a very long time now." Something bordering sadness shadowed her eyes. He wondered about her husband. Where was he when all this was happening to Rachel? Why was she alone at her house?

Alex would give just about anything to ask that and the question foremost in his mind: Did she still hate him for the way he'd ended things between them? He glanced her way. Saw the closed-off expression in her eyes. They weren't there yet. Emotionally, she was on the other side of the earth from him. She'd put up a wall between them that didn't encourage him trying to scale it.

What she didn't realize was that he had been a different man back then. He hadn't believed in anything beyond the job. If he were being honest, he'd known she had wanted out of the Agency for a long time. When their relationship had turned serious, her desire for a normal life seemed to have doubled. Five years ago, Alex couldn't imagine life without the adrenaline rush of the CIA…and so he'd lost her.

"There's a driveway coming up on your right. Turn in there." Rachel's voice interrupted his chaotic thoughts. She didn't look at him, and he wondered if she'd read his thoughts.

He spotted the driveway in question and exited onto a dirt road as dust boiled up in the headlights.

In front of them, an old farmhouse appeared at the end of the drive some distance from the county road.

"Whose place is this?" Alex asked as he stopped the car.

She didn't answer right away and he turned to her, curious.

"This was my husband's family home. He grew up here and I promised him I'd hold on to it after he passed away."

Shocked, Alex couldn't even begin to hide his surprise from her. Nothing prepared him for hearing that Rachel was now a widow. He glanced down at her left ring finger. She still wore her wedding ring. How long had her husband been gone?

Alex looked from her to the simple white house with its pale gray shutters barely distinguishable in the car's headlights. Something akin to jealousy seared his heart. He hated thinking of her loving another man.

Liam had told him she'd gotten married a few years after she'd moved back to Midnight Mountain some five years earlier. After that, well, Alex had just stopped checking in with his friend for a while because it was too painful.

Which was why the envelope he'd received from Liam days before Rachel's call had been so concerning. He had no idea what Liam was trying to convey. It contained ramblings about things they'd done in their childhood and some of the places they'd explored growing up. He assumed Liam had written the letter at a low point. There was no sense in telling Rachel about it and alarming her further.

Alex realized Rachel was staring at him as if she expected him to say something. He pulled himself together and cleared his throat. "I'm sorry. I had no idea your husband had passed away." She continued to stare at him with those telling blue eyes. The look in them now reminded him of when he'd told her he wasn't leaving the CIA with her.

Was she expecting him to be jealous that she'd gotten married? If so, then she should be happy. She had no idea how hard he'd taken the news of her wedding.

"Thank you," she murmured, and looked

away. While a thousand questions flew through his head, he could tell she wasn't ready to discuss any of them with him. "We should probably put the car away and get inside. It's possible that whoever attacked us will connect this place with me." She stopped for a breath. "There's an old garage behind the house. We can hide the car in there."

Once they'd stowed the rental car in the rickety old garage that was a little ways from the house, Alex grabbed his gear and followed her while the dog sniffed around the yard for a bit then went after them, keeping close to Rachel.

Rachel flipped on the lights, illuminating the drop cloths that covered most of the furniture inside the home.

"Sorry for the mess," she told him. "It's just easier to keep clean this way. The place has sat empty for several years now. Brian's family raised workhorses up here for many years. I still keep a few pastured out back because he loved working with them so much. There's a neighbor who stops by each day to care for them."

He managed an awkward nod and dropped his backpack by the door. "I'll take a quick look around just to be safe." He could see she hadn't considered the possibility that the place might not be secure. She'd been away from the spy game too long.

She shook her head and smiled at him for the first time since their reunion. It stopped him dead in his tracks. "I never even considered someone might have already been here."

He loved her smile. He'd almost forgotten just how beautiful she was, especially when she smiled. She wore her golden brown hair longer now. She'd braided it and it hung halfway down her back, the overhead light catching the gold highlights. Dressed in a plaid shirt, jeans and cowboy boots, she reminded him of the young girl he'd fallen for all those years ago. Only her midnight blue eyes held a hint of the things she'd endured. There was a sadness in them that appeared embedded there.

Alex collected his straying thoughts. "Not looking over your shoulder all the time sounds like a good thing. I'll be right back." He excused himself and went upstairs, grateful for the chance to get control of his emotions. He thought he'd left Midnight Mountain behind for good when he went away to college, yet so many of his childhood memories were tied to this place. And to this woman…

After he finished checking the upstairs rooms, he was more ready to join her again. At the foot of the stairs, he noticed that the dog had settled down close to Rachel's feet.

"There's no sign anyone's been up there in a while…" He stopped when he noticed her staring strangely at the desk in the corner of the room. "What is it?"

Rachel visibly shivered. "Even though it's a half hour drive from my home, I still come here every couple of days to make sure the place is okay. I'm pretty sure that drawer was closed when I was here yesterday."

He stared at the desk and then at her. "Someone's been here." He stated the obvious. "What was in there?"

She shook her head. "That's just it. Nothing was in there. There isn't anything of value here besides the horses."

"But they weren't looking for something valuable." Their gazes locked and a new fear entangled him in its clutches. "Whoever was here was looking for something connected to Liam."

No doubt the people behind Liam's disappearance had known about his connection to Rachel all along, including this house.

"You said you keep horses on the property?" Alex's thoughts snarled together. What she'd told him about Liam was disturbing. That Liam had left her the location where he was scheduled to meet his asset seemed to indicate he had been concerned something might happen to him up there.

"That's right. Why?" she asked innocently enough.

"Because they may be our only way out of here." Alex glanced out the front window at the breaking dawn. They'd need to keep moving. Get up on the mountain as soon as possible.

"The stalls are behind the house a little ways down near the south pasture."

"Good. Then we should probably head out. Are you ready for this?" She didn't hesitate. Rachel had been one of the best agents he'd had the pleasure of working with. She might be a little rusty, but she was more than capable.

If something had happened to Liam, each day that passed whittled away at his chances of survival. Rachel said she'd had no word from her brother in more than a week. As a former CIA agent herself, she would know that it was common practice for agents to carry burner phones as a means of communicating without being tracked. If Liam hadn't reached out to her by now, then something bad was wrong.

It bothered Alex that Liam seemed worried about something. It wasn't like his friend to show fear, but from Rachel's account, he'd definitely been concerned when he showed up at her place. He had told her he was close to bringing down a new player in the terror field. He'd mentioned something similar the last time he and Alex had talked.

Did Liam's disappearance have anything to do with what he'd uncovered about the terrorist threat? If so, then whomever he was chasing seemed determined to silence anyone who got in their way or attempted to uncover their identity.

As he and Rachel headed out into the new day dawning, with Callie at their heels, Alex could almost feel her uneasiness growing.

He touched her arm and she slowed her steps and faced him. "We'll find him, I promise. And don't forget, Liam's tough. He's been through much worse than this."

She smiled without answering. Did she believe him?

He needed to get a look at the map. It would give some indication as to where exactly on the mountain they'd be heading. "Do you have the map Liam left you handy?" he asked, and she dug it out of her pocket and handed it to him.

Once he'd opened it, he recognized the location right away. It was more than a twenty-four hike under the best of conditions and over some very rugged terrain.

"This is where Liam was going to meet with his asset?" he asked with a sense of foreboding.

She nodded. "I think so."

Even if they headed straight there, they'd still have to find a place to make camp for the night before hiking the rest of the way up. Darkness came early to the mountains. They'd never make it to the site before nightfall. The weather would definitely play a factor, especially with the mountains making their own conditions. It might be early spring, but snow and ice weren't unexpected this time of year. Up on the mountain several feet of snow still clung to the crevasses.

"I hate going into a situation blind like this, and we don't know for sure what's really happened to Liam. Maybe something went wrong with the meet and he was injured. Or maybe his asset sold him out." Alex glanced around, expecting trouble.

Rachel hesitated a second too long. Right away he could tell something was wrong.

"What is it?" He almost dreaded her answer.

"There's something else I haven't showed you, Alex. It's on the back of the map."

He turned it over and saw the phone number and initial Rachel had mention previously. But it was the words that were scribbled below them that increased his concern for Liam's well-being tenfold.

Agency. Dirty. Trust no one. Especially any-

one in authority. It was a message Liam had intended for Rachel alone.

Alex stared at it and then her. If true, the magnitude of what they now faced had grown beyond anything he could have imagined.

Rachel dragged in a breath before she delivered the worst news possible.

"Alex, I think the person Liam was chasing, this new terrorist threat that he'd uncovered... I think it involves someone from the CIA."

TWO

The expression of shock on his face told her how hard it was for him to wrap his head around the idea that someone from the CIA, both her brother and Alex's own team, might be responsible for harming Liam.

"Rachel…" Her name came out on a frustrated-sounding sigh. Alex couldn't hide his doubts. She certainly understood. As an agent, his head wouldn't let him go there.

"I know how crazy this sounds, but you weren't there when Liam came to see me. He was spooked, and Liam doesn't spook easily. I think his disappearance is in some way connected to the new threat he's been chasing. Maybe he uncovered information that connected someone in the CIA as possibly being involved with this terrorist somehow."

She looked up at him, willing him to understand. "It makes sense, Alex," she said.

Yet he couldn't hide his skepticism. After all,

Alex was still part of the CIA, and there was a bond between agents that was unbreakable. In his mind, it would be unimaginable to think someone you trusted with your life might betray you in such a deadly way.

Still, she tried to make him understand. "Just think about it. Those people who showed up at my house obviously knew about Liam's meet location. They managed to connect my name to Liam, even though it's an alias. They probably knew who he was meeting with as well, and those arrangements are kept confidential for the agent's safety. So how would they possibly know about it without having some inside information?"

His gaze locked on hers; he was clearly surprised by what she'd said. "What are you talking about? You don't know that they knew who Liam was meeting."

Rachel blew out a breath and explained. "I do. I overheard something one of them said. They believe Liam and someone else, probably his asset, are still up on the mountain. Alex, I know you don't want to think it's possible, I didn't either in the beginning, but this is Liam and his life is at stake. We can't afford to discount anything. If they're right and he's somewhere up there still, he could be hurt. He needs our help, because no one else, the CIA included, is going to help him."

Before he could voice his obvious doubts aloud, a noise in the distance captured both their attentions. It sounded like a car on the gravel road nearby slowly coming to a halt.

"That seems really close." She turned her anxious gaze to his.

"You're right. If they've found us again, we'd better hurry." Rachel led the way to the pasture where she kept a couple of mares stalled.

"The horses know this terrain better than I do. They'll get us out of here, but it will be slow going. Do you still remember how to ride?" she asked with a hint of teasing in her tone.

He shook his head, managing a smile for her. "Don't worry about me. I think I can remember well enough to keep up."

The woods expanded into fertile pastureland and Rachel headed toward the barn where the horses were stabled. Behind them, nothing but eerie silence could be heard. Had the car turned around and left already or were they coming after them on foot?

Alex obviously still had concerns. "The sooner we're saddled and riding, the better."

"There are a couple of sleeping bags and some camping gear stored at the back of the barn on a shelf there. We'll need the gear for staying overnight." She pushed open the barn door and went inside. One of the mares neighed when she spotted Rachel.

"It's okay, Naomi." Rachel went over and patted the horse's head. "You ready for a ride?" Next to Naomi, Esther, the second mare, whinnied.

Alex and Rachel worked quickly to saddle the mares and within no time they were leading them out of the barn.

"Let's grab the rest of the supplies from inside," Rachel said. She and Alex went back into the barn and brought out the sleeping bags along with camping gear, then split the load between the two horses. Rachel quickly mounted Naomi and headed down one of the trails behind the house. Alex did the same with Esther.

"There's a ridge not too far from here. It has a great view of the house and the surrounding area. We can get a better idea of what's going on down below," she told him once he'd caught up with her.

Both mares covered the rocky countryside easily enough, with Callie keeping good time behind them. Once they neared the ridge, they dismounted and tied the horses in a treed area some distance from the ridge and hiked the rest of the way up.

Rachel brought out the binoculars that had

been part of the camping gear and homed in on the road near the house.

"The vehicle is parked on the edge of the road close to the driveway. There's no one inside." She frowned as she studied it. "And it's not the same one that was at my house." She handed Alex the binoculars.

"Where are they?" he murmured as he focused on the wooded area between the road and the house. "Wait, I see something." Alex zeroed in on a particular spot.

"What do you see?" She barely got the words out before he turned and grabbed her around the waist. "Get down." Alex tugged her into the shelter of his arms and hit the ground as the world around them exploded with gunfire.

Alex's body protected her from most of the blowback from tree branches splintering and dirt kicking up around them as the bullets hit all around. Close by, Callie whined pitifully and tromped for cover.

"Let's get out of here. There's enough firepower down there to take down a small village. They could have snipers anywhere." The tension in Alex's voice somehow got through the shock that had kept her immobile.

He got to his knees and took her hand. Together they crept as close to the ground as possible until they'd reached the horses.

"Keep as low as you can," he told her as they mounted their horses once more and headed in the opposite direction from the shooters.

Both he and Rachel leaned in close to their horses' necks, almost lying flat against the beasts.

"Can we make it to the base of the mountain riding?" Alex's tone was strained. He glanced back over his shoulder, as if expecting the enemy to emerge behind them at any moment.

Rachel made sure Callie was able to keep up with them. She wouldn't leave the dog behind no matter what.

"Yes, but we'll have to go slower in that rocky terrain, and we will be using up valuable time we don't have to spare. Alex, we need help."

The path widened slightly and he rode up beside her. With no sign of the men behind them, they sat up straight once more. "Who do you suggest?"

In her mind, there was only two people she trusted other than Alex. "The Reagans are my neighbors and good friends. I can call Tom and have him meet us someplace. He can pick up the horses and bring a four-wheeler. We'll make better time with it."

She could tell Alex wasn't nearly as confident in the plan.

"Alex, you can trust them, I promise. They

moved to the area soon after we all went away to the university. I've known them ever since I came back home. They're like family."

He slowly nodded. "If you trust them, so do I. Give them a call. The sooner we get to Liam's meeting location, the faster we'll be able to figure out what happened to him."

The problem was that she had no phone to make the call. "I destroyed both my phone and Liam's right after I called the number he'd written down. I phoned you from my landline. I thought that if what Liam suspected were true, and these people are somehow connected to the CIA, a rogue group of agents perhaps, they'd pull apart my life piece by piece. Probably track his cell or mine. Or both. I couldn't take the chance."

Admiration shone in Alex's eyes. She'd put a lot of thought into destroying the phones, but then, some of her CIA training was still useful.

"Good thinking. Hang on." He pulled out his cell phone and handed it to her. "Use this one. It's a burner phone and no one knows the number."

She smiled her gratitude and dialed her friend's number while praying that whoever was chasing them hadn't contacted her neighbor already.

The short amount of time it took Tom to answer did little to settle her nerves.

"Tom, it's Rachel. I need you to meet me at Willow Creek as soon as possible. And bring the four-wheeler."

"I should be able to do that," Tom said in an evasive tone that made her wonder if someone was listening in on the conversation.

Rachel glanced uneasily at Alex. "I'll meet you there in a couple of hours, then." After a second of silence on his end, she told Tom goodbye and then ended the call. She handed the phone back to Alex while praying she wasn't leading the enemy right to them.

"He's on his way. Willow Creek is due north of here. There's some pretty hilly areas between, but we should be able to make it in an hour." She hesitated. "Alex, Tom sounded strange, almost as if someone were there and he couldn't talk."

Rachel could see right away that he didn't like it. "You think they're watching him?"

She shook her head. "I don't know, but we'd better check out the area around Willow Creek very carefully when we get there. We could have unwanted company."

The trail was just wide enough for the two of them to ride side by side for a bit and, thankfully, it was mostly level.

"Where will this trail take us?" Alex asked, keeping a careful eye on the surrounding woods.

"It will dump us out at Willow Creek after we summit Plume Mountain."

She couldn't help it; she had to look at him. His gaze tangled with hers. She could see that he remembered the place, as well. They'd once spent a lot of time hiking the valley below Plume Mountain and fishing back when it had been her, Liam and Alex. Before life got complicated and their career paths took them through troubled waters.

"When was the last time you spoke to Liam?" Rachel asked, mostly because she needed a distraction to get his attention off her so that she could reclaim some of her equilibrium.

There was something in Alex's gaze that drew her in and made her wonder if he, too, was remembering their time here together. Back then their romance was just beginning. They had skirted around the edges of their feelings since they were teens. She'd often wondered what her younger self would have done if only she'd known the outcome.

"Too long ago, I'm afraid." He clearly regretted the lapse. "I'd like to say we both got busy, but I guess in truth it was just too hard." He spared her a look and she swallowed with difficulty and looked away, her heart going crazy with possibilities. Did Alex have regrets about their parting? He certainly hadn't showed it all those years ago.

When Rachel had made up her mind to get out, she hadn't realized how hard it would be. Hadn't known she'd be walking away from Alex along with the Agency. She'd been a broken person when she came back to her hometown of Midnight Mountain. She'd spent weeks crying. Liam had tried his best to console her, but Liam was cut from the same cloth as Alex. They both ate, breathed and slept the CIA.

For a long time, Rachel hadn't known what to do to move on beyond Alex. She'd gone to church with the Reagans one Sunday. She had felt a sense of peace that day, realizing that she wasn't alone in her pain. Knowing that God was with her no matter what happened in her life. It was because of this that her heart had begun to mend.

"To tell you the truth—" Alex's familiar voice interrupted her unsettled thoughts "—I've missed working with Liam…and you."

Her heart contracted painfully and she struggled to keep from showing how hard it was to hear him say those things. Why was he telling her this *now*?

She'd buried how handsome he was deep in her heart. Now it was a painful reminder of the dreams she'd given up. He was tall and fit; his dark brown hair now almost touched his collar. Those piercing green eyes still held a hint of mischief in them whenever he smiled, as they had when they were kids growing up together. Yet the years and the job had left their mark on him. Fine lines fanned out around his eyes and mouth. She'd witnessed enough horror in her years on the job to know the reason behind those lines.

Rachel shoved those dark memories back into the recesses of her heart. She needed to keep her focus on her brother.

"I called Liam a couple of months back," Alex said, surprising her. "He didn't answer, but he called me back a little after from a phone number I didn't recognize. For some reason, the number stuck in my head."

He gave it to her. She didn't recognize it, either. She shook her head. "I've never heard him use that number before."

Alex nodded. "Anyway, we talked for a bit. He sounded…tired. Distracted, maybe. He said he was getting ready to leave on a mission to Iraq."

She remembered the time. "You're right. Liam was distracted back then. Actually, for a while. At first, I wasn't so worried. You know how Liam throws himself into his mission to the point of being consumed by it. But his behavior became increasingly more withdrawn as the weeks went by. Then he showed up at my house…and you know the rest." She shrugged. "I think Iraq was just a staging location, though. He was heading behind enemy lines."

"It makes sense. The fewer people who know about where an agent is going, the better chance they have of surviving. The last time we talked, he told me a little of the same things he told you. About this new player coming onto his radar. He seemed really worried and alluded to the fact that if they couldn't find out his identity soon, it could have deadly consequences."

Rachel shivered at the implication. Had Liam tracked the identity of the person and found out it was one of his own people?

As they rode along, a tree branch snapped close to the edge of the trail, immediately drawing Rachel's attention back to the moment. Was it just an innocent animal roaming the woods nearby? Or had an enemy found them and was closing in quickly?

Alex reined in his mare and listened carefully. Nothing but silence followed. The sound had come from just up ahead. Slowly, he dismounted and drew his weapon. Rachel did the same.

Close by, the dog growled and headed for

the woods in the direction of the sound, sniffing the air.

"Stay, Callie," Rachel ordered and stopped the dog with that verbal command. Callie sat back on her haunches, her guard up.

"Stay behind me," Alex said and then eased into the treed area. Once inside, he stopped for a second to take stock. At one time, he had known these woods like the back of his hand. He and Liam had hunted just about everything the forest provided since they were kids. Alex could recognize the different sounds made by animals that roamed the mountains, and the noise he'd just heard earlier didn't belong to any of those animals.

To the right, another twig snapped, riveting both their attentions that way. A mule deer stood frozen in place not far from the spot, staring at them. Rachel let go of a breath, relieved. Yet Alex couldn't share in it, because he was positive the previous sound hadn't come from the deer.

Rachel turned to look at him and saw the truth in his eyes. He barely had time to shake his head before something charged from the bushes nearby and right for them.

A man dressed completely in black, with a ski mask covering his face, hit Alex full force before he had time to react.

The momentum of the man broadsiding him sent both of them sprawling across the rocky ground. Alex's weapon flew from his hand. The man had slung an assault rifle behind his back.

As Alex struggled for control, his attacker temporarily gained the upper hand, and they wrestled back and forth. In the hand-to-hand combat that ensued, the man's assault rifle slipped off his arm. They were now both unarmed. Alex was relying on physical strength alone.

Out of the corner of his eye, Alex saw Rachel struggling to get a clear shot off. With them grappling back and forth, there was no opportunity.

Alex managed to free one hand and he slugged his attacker hard. The man's head spun sideways and he yelped in pain. The fury in his eyes was pure evil as he clutched Alex around the throat, trying to strangle him. Alex fought free and punched the man hard once more. This time, he slumped to the side, stunned by the blow. It was enough for Alex to get away. Jumping to his feet, he searched the ground for his Glock. He recalled the general direction it had landed, but it was nowhere in sight.

Rachel fired off a warning shot as Alex's attacker regained his senses. "Stay where you are," she ordered. The man didn't listen.

Before Alex located the weapon, the man lunged for him once more. This time Alex was prepared. He set his feet and grabbed hold of the man's arms.

His assailant was yelling at the top of his lungs. It wouldn't be long before his buddies zeroed in on the direction of the noise and came to his aid.

Before Alex could slug the man again, Rachel slammed the stock of her gun hard against the man's temple. He didn't have time to register what had happened before he slumped to the ground at Alex's feet.

It took a second for Alex to gather his breath and then he knelt next to the man. Yanking the mask off, he recoiled when he got a good look at him. He recognized the man from somewhere.

"Do you know him?" Rachel asked in amazement, seeing his reaction.

"I'm not sure." A quick search of his pockets produced a driver's license with the man's name on it. Alex wasn't sure what he'd been expecting. Certainly not that something about the man's face would be familiar. The name, on the other hand, was elusive. He stared down at the man, racking his brain to come up with how he might know him, but he just couldn't place it.

Alex handed the ID to Rachel. "It says his

name is Victor McNamara. Does it ring a bell to you?"

She studied the photo for a second, then shook her head and handed it back to Alex. He shoved it in his pocket and then slung the assault rifle over his shoulder.

"Let's go. The way he was carrying on, everyone within a two-mile radius will have heard him."

They hurried past the waiting dog, who leaped to her feet. Once they were both back in the saddle, Rachel nudged the mare forward, and Alex followed.

While the horses made their way across the uneven countryside, Alex tried to make sense of what had just taken place. Why did this man look familiar? He was positive he recognized him from somewhere. He needed to figure out where and soon. Their lives and Liam's depended on it.

The fact that they were coming after Rachel with such force gave him some hope that Liam might still be alive and had gotten away somehow. They'd need her to find her brother. Yet if Liam were still up on Midnight Mountain and if he was hurt, he could be in danger from more than just the men hunting him. The temperature at night up at the higher altitude could plunge well below freezing.

On the back of the capable mare Esther, Alex took in the passing countryside as they steadily climbed. It amazed him that through it all, Callie kept a careful stride behind them. The dog reminded him a lot of a mutt he'd had as a kid. He'd loved that dog until the day she'd passed away.

Alex took a second to gain his bearings. They were almost to the top of Plume Mountain, one of the many mountains neighboring Midnight Mountain.

He couldn't figure out how Victor McNamara or any of the events that had taken place related to Liam's disappearance. He was positive the name was a fake.

Frustrated, Alex shook his head. It was beyond him at the moment. Right now, with the steady climb, it took all his skills and concentration to keep on the mare.

After they'd put sufficient distance between themselves and the men hunting them, Rachel slowed the horse's speed and Alex caught up to her.

Her brown hair was windblown. Her cheeks flushed from the ride. And she had never looked more beautiful to him…or more worried.

"Are you okay?" Alex asked when he got a good look at her expression.

She shrugged. "I don't know anymore. What

was that about back there, Alex? Why do these people want us dead? And why is someone trying to kill Liam? Liam is a patriot. He would never compromise his loyalty to our country for anything. So, if those men are CIA, why do they want him dead?"

"I don't think it's a matter of Liam compromising his values, but someone else compromising theirs. That man back there, to name one. I'm not sure what Liam uncovered, but he's in serious danger because of it." He hesitated before voicing his concerns. "Rachel, we can't do this alone, especially when we really don't know what we're up against. We could both end up dead. Let me call in my team." He pressed when she didn't answer. "I promise we can trust them."

She stared at him as if he had lost his mind. "We can't. Even if we can trust your team, who's to say that someone won't mention what's happening here to a colleague? We could all end up dead because of it. Please, we can't reach out to anyone connected to the CIA."

He understood her reluctance was because of what Liam had scribbled on the back of the map, but that didn't change the fact that they were grossly outnumbered.

"All right, I'll go along with it for now, but the sooner we get some breathing room between us and those thugs back there, the better." He expelled a weary sigh.

She smiled over at him and squeezed his arm. "Thank you, Alex. And thank you for coming so soon. I know it couldn't have been easy."

To be honest, he hadn't even thought about it. He'd just come. Her call had left him shaken. He'd gone against every instinct screaming inside of him that told him he was making a bad decision by not looping in his CIA Scorpion commander, Jase Bradford. He'd simply left Jase in the dark as to why he needed a few days off for personal time. Then he'd borrowed his buddy Aaron Foster's plane and left Colorado right away, because something had happened to Liam and Rachel needed him.

"You know I'd do anything for Liam and for you. You guys are like family." He watched her draw in a breath, her eyes clouding with some unnamed emotion he'd give anything to understand. There was a time when he knew what her every little expression meant. Back before he'd screwed things up.

"We should probably keep going. They could have men stationed farther up this mountain," she murmured, looking away, breaking the spell.

Before he could answer, Rachel nudged the mare and headed up the trail once more. After a moment, he followed, while rebuking himself over letting his emotions get the better of him. He had to stay focused. The past was over and done. He was here for Liam.

So far, it didn't appear that anyone was following them, but Rachel was right. They could have men everywhere. Until they had a better handle on what they faced, they needed to stay on the move. They'd be harder to track that way.

It took more than a heart-pounding hour before they summited the top of Plume Mountain, one of the lesser mountains that was part of a chain of them stretching through the area. There was still a long ways to travel before they reached their destination of Midnight Mountain. Rachel reined to a stop and took out the binoculars once more to scan the area below them where Willow Creek was located before handing them to him.

"I don't see anything. Not even Tom." She got off the horse and stretched out the kinks in her back.

After he'd checked the area and was satisfied they were safe for the moment, he did the same back stretches. He had finally gotten a sense of where he was again. He'd been away for years. It took a while to reacquaint.

"He should have been here long before us. I don't see his truck and trailer." She turned to

Alex. "I don't like it. What if he was being held hostage? What if they followed him here?"

He went over to where she stood and placed his hands on her shoulders. He could feel her grow tense in reaction to his touch and he hid his hurt with difficulty.

"Hey, we don't know anything's happened yet," he said, and yet as much as he tried to reassure her, Rachel was right. By vehicle, the drive shouldn't take more than a half hour.

"Where would he normally park?" he asked while trying not to show his concern. If these people were somehow CIA, they'd have the full resources of the Agency at their disposal. They could make people disappear...for good.

She pointed to some trees close to a trailhead. "Tom and his wife come here quite often. When my husband was alive, he and I would ride horses with them up here. Tom always parked over there."

The mention of her husband was a painful reminder of the things that could have been his. He found himself being jealous of a dead man. Pitiful.

"Let's not think the worst until we know for sure. Anything could have happened. A flat tire. Maybe it took him longer to load the four-wheeler than usual." Alex tried to sound positive, but his worst fear was that the men coming after them had gotten to Rachel's friend.

"Wait, I see something." She pointed down below, then took up the binoculars once more. "That's him. But he's riding the four-wheeler... I thought he would pull it on a trailer behind his truck," she said with a bewildered frown. "Something's not right."

Rachel headed back to the horses, ready to ride down into the valley, but he stopped her.

"Hang on a second. We still don't know if he's here alone or by his own will, for that matter. Like you said, something's not right."

She stared at him for the longest time. "There's no way Tom would set us up."

He didn't break eye contact. "Maybe not willingly, but he may not have had a choice."

She drew in a breath. "All right. What do you suggest we do?"

He scanned the area below them once again. "Let's leave the horses up here and go the rest of the way down on foot." Alex pointed to the left. "There's plenty of tree coverage through there. If there's someone else with him, we'll be better able to take them by surprise."

"Okay," she agreed, and then led the mares into the woods to find a location where they could tie them off with plenty of grass for grazing.

Once they'd strapped on their backpacks,

with Callie glued to their heels, Alex took the lead. "Stay close to me and if anything happens, get back here and ride out as fast as you can," he told her, knowing she wouldn't do any of those things. She was a soldier at heart and a soldier would never leave a fellow comrade behind.

The hike down the opposite side of the mountain proved just as treacherous as the summit had. All the while, Alex couldn't get the man who had attacked him out of his head. Was he CIA? They were sworn to protect, but it wouldn't be unheard of for one of their own to go rogue. Still, why come after Liam unless he'd uncovered the traitorous threat? Was it possible this new terrorist had gotten Liam involved in something way over his head?

Once they reached the valley, Alex stopped long enough to bring out the binoculars and scan the area. There didn't appear to be anyone else around but the man who had dismounted the four-wheeler and stood looking around with a rifle in his hand.

The dog had stuck close to them the whole way down, as if sensing something was off.

"I don't see anyone but your friend." He drew his weapon and turned to her. "Just in case," he said in response to her raised brow.

They stepped from the cover of the trees close to the man with the four-wheeler who stood at full alert. His body language alone seemed to confirm something had gone wrong.

Callie spotted Tom and galloped toward him, tail wagging. A twig snapped beneath the dog's paw and the man whirled at the sound, shotgun ready to fire.

The moment he spotted Rachel, he visibly relaxed, then reached down and patted the dog's head. When he saw Alex with a gun in his hand, his demeanor changed immediately. He clutched the rifle tighter. Alex had no doubt he was skilled at using it.

"It's okay, Tom. He's my friend," Rachel said, and then rushed over to give the man a heartfelt hug.

Alex watched her with the older man and it was easy to see that she loved him.

She stepped back and turned to Alex. "Tom, this is Alex Booth. We grew up here together. He and Liam are good friends."

Alex tucked the Glock behind his back and shook the man's hand. "Good to meet you, sir."

"You, too," Tom said with a firm handshake. He watched as the dog went to explore a nearby plant. Alex could tell the man seemed distracted by something.

"Has something happened, Tom?" Rachel obviously saw the same thing he did.

After a moment or two of silence, Tom looked

at Rachel. "I wasn't able to bring the truck. I used the four-wheeler to slip out the back way." The man shook his head. "I'm not really sure what to make of it, but it scared me. I haven't seen anything like it in my seventy-plus years."

He paused for a breath and Rachel shot Alex a worried glance.

"Right before you called, a couple of men showed up at my place asking a whole bunch of questions about Liam and you." The concern in Tom's eyes was real enough. "They had IDs." He shook his head. "They said they worked for the CIA… Rachel, they said Liam did something terrible. They said he wants to hurt a lot of people."

All the color drained from Rachel's face. "That's not true. Tom, you know it's not true. Liam would never hurt anyone."

Tom's expression softened and he managed a smile for her. "I know that. I'd trust Liam with my life. Jenny, too. But these men seemed determined to lay the blame on him for something. They said he betrayed his country." Tom spat the words out and shook his head. "Jenny was in the kitchen when they showed up. I wasn't going to let them inside, but they pretty much forced their way in. Something about them just worried me. When you called, I went in the other room. That's why I couldn't talk much."

He stopped for a second. "Anyway, Jenny told me after they'd gone that she's pretty sure she saw at least a half dozen more men in the woods surrounding the house. They were coming from the direction of your place. She said they were armed to the teeth."

He blew out an uneven breath. "They're coming after you, too, Rachel. And they're not going to stop until they find you and Liam. And I don't think they care if that's dead or alive."

THREE

It felt as if the ground had been yanked out from beneath her feet. Was it possible that this whole thing was all about someone trying to frame Liam for a crime they had committed? What were they trying to cover up?

"You saw their IDs? They were definitely CIA?" she asked in shock.

Callie trotted back from her exploring as if sensing her owner's unease.

Tom nodded. "I did. They looked like CIA to me, or a very good forgery."

Alex pulled out the driver's license they'd taken from the man who attacked them. "Is this one of the men you spoke with?"

Tom took the ID and studied it before shaking his head. "Nope, that's not one of them. The two who did the talking were both dark-haired. Average looks. Around the same age as this guy, though. They were definitely trying to be intimidating and let me say, they accomplished it." He handed the ID back to Alex.

Perplexed, Rachel turned to Alex. "It could be the same man from this morning. Was one of them injured?" she asked Tom.

Tom appeared alarmed. "No, at least not that I could tell. What happened this morning?" His concern was obvious. Rachel gave him the amended version.

He shook his head. "Unbelievable. I told Jenny I thought I heard shots pretty early this morning. I'm sorry I didn't come to your aid, Rachel."

She patted his arm. "I'm glad you didn't. They might have killed you."

That chilling reality hung between them, keeping everyone silent for a while.

"Still no word from Liam?" Tom asked, breaking the quiet.

"No." And she was terrified for Liam's well-being, especially after what the man who broke into her house had said. She had no idea how many days her brother had actually been missing or if the person he'd gone there to meet had set him up. The only information she had was where he was going, a dangerous location near the top of Midnight Mountain.

"Do you need me to help with the search?" Tom

asked, and his generous offer came as no surprise even though she knew she couldn't accept.

"Thank you, Tom, but it's too dangerous. We'll be okay." Rachel wished she felt as confident as those words sounded.

Tom bowed his head. He had been so protective of her since Brian's passing.

Alex touched her arm. "I hate to say it, but we should probably get going. Those men know the general direction we're heading. They'll keep coming after us."

She swallowed deeply. She hated to let Tom go. Would she see him again?

Please, God...

"You're right." She faced the older man again. "We left the horses up on top of the mountain." She didn't want to leave them in the elements too long.

"Don't worry about it. Callie and I will fetch them and take them home with me," Tom assured her. "You two get going. The less time spent out in the open like this, the better. Jenny packed you food in the four-wheeler's storage compartment."

Tom stared at her for a long time with worry creasing his face. She knew he was concerned for her safety and so she tried to ease his mind.

"We'll be okay, I promise. Thank you for

the use of the four-wheeler. And thank Jenny, as well."

Tom and Jenny had been like family to her since her own parents passed away three years ago. Without them and Liam, she wouldn't have gotten through losing her husband.

After years in the trenches of a different and terrifying kind of warfare, Rachel had thought she'd left behind the dangerous life she'd once led. Yet here she was right back in the thick of it again, and suddenly she wasn't so sure she could survive this time.

She hugged Tom one more time, hating to leave him, but Alex was right. Tom needed to get home to Jenny and they'd need to put distance between themselves and the men hunting them. And she had no idea what they'd face once they got up on the mountain.

"Be careful, Tom. Those men could still be close and watching your place."

Tom stood up a little taller. "Jenny stayed behind in case they came back with more questions. She thought it might look suspicious if we were both gone. She's a better shot than I am and can handle herself in any situation. If they know what's best for them, they'll steer clear of her. And don't worry about me. I know this countryside better than anyone. I'll give them the slip if they're still hanging around my property. You two just watch your backs."

Alex pulled out a piece of paper and wrote something down. "If anything comes up and you feel threatened, call this number. Ask for Jase Bradford. Tell him what's happened and he'll send help right away. He's a friend and you can trust him," Alex said, and she believed it was just as much for her benefit as for Tom's.

"I will." Tom put the number in his shirt pocket and then hugged Rachel once more. "Stay safe. And find Liam."

"We will." She drew in an emotional-riddled breath and turned to Alex. "It's been a while since you've been up on the mountain. Do you mind if I drive?"

He smiled at her and some long-suppressed memory resurfaced of a time they'd spent together on a moonlit night. He'd looked at her much in the same way. She'd been crazy about him back then. She still loved the way he smiled.

"I'm fine with that. In fact, I'm happy to act as lookout. But the sooner we get on our way, the better. We have a long trip ahead of us, and this machine can only take us so far."

She got on the four-wheeler and he hopped on behind her. Suddenly having him so close was a little too unsettling. It reminded her of all the times they'd spent in each other's company in the past, both here and in the field. It made her want to protect her heart from the inevitable time when he left her again…and he would.

They were still some distance from Midnight Mountain. With a final wave to Tom, Rachel headed the machine off in the same direction her friend had entered the valley.

The four-wheeler's powerful engine took the steep incline easily enough, but Rachel was concerned that once they reached the higher altitudes, the snow and ice would make it a dangerous trek. They'd be on foot and vulnerable. She just hoped the weather held.

They said Liam did something terrible…

There was no way she'd ever believe her brother would hurt anyone without cause. So why was someone so determined to brand Liam a traitor? What exactly had he uncovered?

If someone from the CIA was a double agent, then they'd stop at nothing to keep their crimes from being uncovered, and chances were, they hadn't acted alone.

Alex leaned forward so that she could hear him over the roar of the engine. "We may have a bigger problem. There's no way we can conceal the noise this thing makes. And the location where Liam indicated on the map is close to nine thousand feet in altitude."

Rachel had considered the same thing, too.

"You're right. We'll need to find a place to leave it once we reach the base of Midnight Mountain. How are you at hiking these days?"

When they were younger, the three of them had hiked this mountain dozens of times. There was one spot in particular that they loved to camp at. The mountains at night were breathtaking and the stars appeared close enough to touch.

Alex chucked softly, the sound sending chills through her nervous system. "Don't worry. I'm not that out of shape. I think I can still keep up with you."

He certainly appeared fit enough. Outdoorsy as ever, Alex would always be the most handsome man she knew. Yet being close to him brought up emotions she'd just as soon not deal with.

She'd been crazy about him for as long as she could remember. The three of them had been determined to stay close after high school, and so they'd attended the same university. Deciding to join the CIA had been a joint decision, as well. They had all excelled at the job...for a while.

But soon, the stress of the life of an agent became too much for Rachel. Her world consisted of one dangerous mission followed by another. She found herself needing more than the adrenaline rush. She wanted a life beyond the spy games they played. A family. And she wanted all those things with Alex. She just hadn't expected his reaction. He didn't share any of her dreams.

Now, Rachel found herself wondering about what his life had been like over the past five years. Liam had told her that Alex had taken a different job within the CIA, a more specialized detachment, but he hadn't been able to talk about it much. Was Alex involved with someone new, or was he still married to the job?

Somehow, Rachel let go of the past. No sense crying over spilled milk. Neither one of them could go back in time and change things.

"We're almost to the base." Her voice sounded less than steady. It was just the past. It had a way of coming to the surface no matter how hard she tried to keep it buried. Right now, she had to find a way to shove it aside. She needed Alex's help to bring her brother home.

"There's a group of scrub brush to your left. They'll make for a good cover for the machine." Alex pointed to the left side and she eased the four-wheeler in that direction.

When they were close, Alex got off and she followed. They pushed the four-wheeler behind the scrubs and then piled extra brush all around until it was completely obscured from view.

Rachel watched as Alex slipped into his backpack. Just seeing him back home made all of her young girl wishes resurface. She turned away and grabbed the extra backpack filled with supplies and then opened the storage compartment on the four-wheeler and smiled at the sack full of sandwiches, chips, fruit and water Jenny had packed.

Alex came over to where she stood and peered over her shoulder. "Looks like a feast. Remind me to thank her in person when we get back." The words were out before he really thought about them and their eyes locked. Would they make it out of this thing alive?

As she looked into his eyes, Rachel fought to keep her equilibrium. She couldn't get sucked back into Alex's charm again. He was her past. If they survived this, perhaps they'd be able to resume their friendship, but that was all it could ever be.

She wasn't ready for anything more after losing Brian. Even though they both knew his death was inevitable when they'd married, losing him had still brought her to her knees emotionally. There wasn't anything left inside her to give to someone else, and she couldn't put the pain and heartache Alex had caused her in the past aside, no matter how hard she tried.

The wind kicked up. On it Rachel caught the

faintest of sounds. Voices? Multiple ones. Some-one else was up here.

Before she could get the words out, Alex heard what she did. He pulled her close and whispered, "We need to get out of sight." He glanced around the area. "Over there. A small opening in the mountain. It might be enough to keep us out of their view."

They hurried over to the entrance, looking into what appeared to be a pitch-black gap in the side of the mountain.

"I don't think it's a cave as much as a small crevice," Alex said in a low voice before they stepped inside. He took out his phone and shone the light into the five-foot-deep mountain flaw. "It's not much. If they're paying attention, we'll be sitting ducks. Let's hope that doesn't happen. Here, get on the other side of me." He tugged her deeper into the crevice and as far away from the entrance as possible.

Rachel could feel her heart echoing in her ears. She glanced up and saw Alex watching her. He was probably wondering if she was up to the task at hand.

"Do you think we hid the four-wheeler well enough?" She whispered her concern aloud. If the men spotted the machine, they'd know someone else was up here. If they were deliberately searching for them, then she and Alex wouldn't stand a chance.

"Unless they're really looking, it'll be fine. The camo paint on the machine will help it blend."

She said a prayer in her head as outside, multiple rocks dislodged and rolled down the path. Someone was close. It took everything inside her not to react.

Alex drew her close. She held her breath. More footsteps followed, too many to count. It sounded as if they'd stopped just outside the crevice.

Rachel remembered that they'd forgotten to cover their footsteps. Would the men look down and spot them? If so, they'd know they were right under their noses.

Outside, a cell phone rang. A man answered it. "Yeah." He sounded less than thrilled.

Alex held her closer and she hugged him tight.

"There's no sign of them here. The noise could have been coming from the adjoining cattle ranch. We're heading back your way again," the man said in a sharp tone.

Rachel waited until the men had moved away and it was quiet outside, then she let go of the breath she'd held on to. "They didn't see the four-wheeler, but that was close."

"I counted at least five sets of footsteps." Alex glanced down at her in the darkness. She could almost feel his tension. "I don't understand what's going on here, but I sure hope we find Liam and get some answers soon."

"Me, too. Do you think it's safe to get out?"

"Let me take a quick look around first. Wait here." He slowly slipped out and she felt his absence completely in the oppressing darkness.

Her pulse hammered every single second Alex was gone. When he returned, she resisted the urge to hug him again.

"It looks as if they're heading back toward Plume Mountain, probably to your husband's place. I'm hoping the rest of them are still there."

Rachel followed him out again and stared up at the mountain, which was partially hidden by cloud coverage. A chill sped up her spine.

Where are you, Liam?

In the past, she and her brother always had a special connection. She could almost sense his presence in her heart. Rachel didn't feel him now. She was terrified they were already too late.

"It'll be dark soon. We need to find a place to get out of the elements. We're almost to Midnight Valley. We can camp there and head out again in the morning," Alex told her after they'd been hiking for hours. He felt the exhaustion of the miles they'd covered, fueled by his fear for Liam's safety, catching up with him.

Rachel appeared ready to drop, as well. His heart went out to her. He loved Liam like a brother, but Liam was her flesh and blood. She probably hadn't gotten any sleep since Liam's disappearance.

They reached the top of the peak that looked down on Midnight Valley. The moon had slipped from its cloud coverage and made an appearance for the first time. He could see Midnight Lake in the middle of the valley below them.

Alex lifted up a prayer of thanks for their safe passage so far. They'd battled rough terrain and fear all the way to this point.

Rachel stopped next to him and their gazes held. Alex found himself unable to look away. Even worn-out and disheveled, she was lovely. An old memory from the past resurfaced. The three of them had been chasing an arms dealer for months near Kabul. They'd finally tracked the man's location to a mountainous region in Afghanistan. Alex remembered the area had reminded him of this place. The air had been crackling with electrical tension back then. It was the first time Rachel mentioned leaving the Agency. He'd seen her fear. Realized the toll the job had taken on her. At the time, he couldn't fathom walking away. Now, after being with the specialized CIA Scorpion team for several years, he understood. The team was close and they were doing good things. It wasn't about the high for him anymore. Even so, there were times when he could almost imagine himself back here living in the small town of Midnight Mountain again.

Unexpectedly, he took her hand, and she froze briefly before turning to him. Her blue eyes were huge pools in the moonlight. The unasked questions were all there, and he couldn't bring himself to answer a single one of them.

Through the years, there hadn't been a day that had gone by where he hadn't regretted letting her go. Now, he realized it was too late for them. He'd lost her for good. They weren't the same people they once were.

He squeezed her hand and then let her go and cleared away the regret from his throat. "We'd best keep going. We're going to need to make a fire to stay warm. It's getting colder by the minute."

Something bordering disappointment shadowed her eyes before she nodded and headed down the steep mountainside. After a second, he followed.

Once they reached the valley, Alex glanced

around for the best spot to build a fire without it being seen by anyone above.

He pointed to a treed area. "Let's set up camp over there."

Alex took off his backpack and leaned it against a tree. "I'll gather some wood. Let's get a fire going and then dive into those sandwiches Jenny made. I'm starving."

With the beetle infestation of recent years, there was plenty of dead timber around. Alex gathered an armful and found a good spot for the fire.

Once it was roaring, he and Rachel unrolled their sleeping bags and Rachel took out the food and handed him a sandwich and some chips along with a drink.

"There's fruit if you want some." She took a bite of her sandwich.

Alex didn't answer. He said a prayer of thanksgiving in his head and then dug into his meal with relish. A simple ham sandwich had never tasted so good.

Rachel must have spotted his reaction because she laughed. "It's the mountain air. It makes everything taste better."

He put down his sandwich and watched her. "I remember. All those picnic lunches we used to enjoy. Good times." He swallowed back his regret. He'd give anything to go back to that simpler period in his life.

Alex studied her expression in the firelight. He could almost swear he saw her blush.

She brushed a crumb from her mouth. "They were good times, weren't they? When I first left the CIA and came back home, I used to come up here all the time. I think it was just being in touch with something I loved from childhood that helped ground me."

He understood. He felt the same way.

Alex hesitated, needing to tell her something that could prove touchy. He hadn't been completely honest with her when she'd asked about the last time he'd had contact from Liam. For unknown reasons, he'd chosen not to mention the strange letter he'd received from his friend. Now, more than ever, they needed answers. Maybe something about it might make sense to her.

Alex stared at the fire, unsure of how she would take this new piece of news. "I need to tell you something, Rachel." He glanced her way. Immediately he could see he had her full attention. "A few days before you called, I received a letter in the mail from Liam." Alex stopped and shook his head. "I don't know what to make of it. It's nothing but ramblings to me. Liam talked about our childhood here in Midnight Mountain and some of the places we used to explore together. One in particular is underlined."

Alex took out the letter and handed it to her. When he'd gotten her call, he'd shoved the letter inside his jacket pocket and brought it with him. She unfolded it and read through it, a tear slipping slowly down her cheek.

"I have no idea what he's talking about," she whispered sadly, and then handed him the letter back. He tucked it back in his pocket, the desire to comfort her running deep. Alex reached over and touched her face gently, brushing aside the tears.

Before he could voice the regrets of his heart, a noise close by had them both jumping to their feet, weapons drawn.

A woman and man emerged from the shadowy woods. The woman spotted their weapons right away and quickly raised her hands.

"Oh…we're so sorry. We didn't mean to frighten the two of you. We just lost our way in the dark. When I saw the fire, I was so relieved," the woman said with the tiniest of giggles, her voice accented.

Dressed in dark clothing, she was tall, almost six feet. She stepped closer and Alex got a better look. Her dark hair was pulled back in a ponytail; she wore a baseball cap that covered part of her face.

The man hung back a little ways in the shadows. He held his hands up, too. There was something familiar about him, too, and an uneasy feeling sped through Alex. What was going on here?

Alex moved closer to Rachel's side in a protective gesture that came naturally. "It's okay. We just weren't expecting company tonight." Like her, Alex hadn't lowered his weapon yet.

"We're really sorry to bother you, but would it be okay if we camped out with you tonight? We're both exhausted and I promise we won't be any trouble."

There was something in the woman's voice he couldn't place. Fear. Some type of warning. He was unsure, but Rachel's reaction to hearing the woman speak triggered all sorts of alarms. Was it possible that she recognized the woman?

Rachel reached out and clasped Alex's hand, squeezing it once, then letting go. She was definitely trying to warn him of something.

"Why don't you both come warm yourself by the fire?" Alex said when Rachel stood, silently assessing the woman.

The woman glanced oddly at Rachel, almost as if she knew her. She moved over to the fire and warmed her hands. After a brief hesitation, her partner joined her.

Once Alex got a closer look at the man, he was positive he recognized him. He had no idea how.

Slowly Alex lowered his weapon. Rachel did the same and the woman let out a breath, relieved.

"Sorry to draw down on you like that. We thought you might be a bear." Alex came up with the best explanation he could.

The woman smiled again, but it didn't seem sincere. "No problem. I'm Michelle Mullins, by the way. This is my husband, Peter. We're from Colorado. We've been hiking all the mountains in the Midnight Mountain Range."

Alex strove for calm and eventually found it. He held out his hand and she shook it. Her husband wasn't nearly as friendly.

The woman turned to him. "Peter, shake the man's hand. They're keeping us from freezing to death," she said with another laugh.

The two seemed to be communicating something to each other. After another second, the man smiled and took Alex's hand. "Nice to meet you both."

"You, too," Rachel said with an attempt at a smile once he'd shook her hand.

"Thank you so much for saving us. We got

caught up in the spectacular views from the top of Midnight Mountain and lost track of the time. A foolish mistake, I know." Michelle shook her head. "And one I'm embarrassed to say we made. We've been hiking for years. You'd think we'd know better."

Rachel's gaze met Alex's briefly. He could see she was troubled.

"It's no problem," she said. "Are you two hungry?"

The woman smiled genuinely. "Starving. I'm afraid I didn't pack enough food for the evening meal. I wasn't expecting to be up here." She shrugged.

"It's okay. We have plenty." Rachel brought out some extra sandwiches and a bottle of water and handed them to Michelle.

"Thanks." She took it and gave Peter one of the sandwiches.

"It's easy to get lost up here at night if you're not careful," Alex told the two while keeping a close eye on Peter. Where did he know the man from?

Peter nodded without answering and took a bite from the sandwich.

"Do you guys have sleeping bags with you?" Rachel asked, and looked around at the gear they carried.

From the looks of it, they had prepared for a long stay in spite of what Michelle had said.

"We do. It just makes good sense to be ready." Michelle unzipped her backpack and brought out a sleeping bag. Alex caught a glimpse of what looked like a pistol before she closed the bag again.

He wondered why such knowledgeable hikers would allow themselves to get lost at night. Their story didn't add up.

"So what did you say you did for a living, Alex?" Michelle asked, pinning him with her sharp gaze.

"I didn't." Alex didn't elaborate. He wasn't even trying to pretend anymore. These people were not who they said they were, and his mind had already begun to try to figure out a way to get Rachel and himself out of there safely.

How had they known where to find them? Not for a second did he buy they'd been atop the mountain. He believed they'd been deliberately searching for him and Rachel. The path Alex and Rachel were on wasn't the most direct way to the meet location. In fact, only the locals knew about Midnight Valley, so they didn't just happen here by accident.

"We should probably get some more firewood," Alex told Rachel. "We don't want the fire to go out overnight. Why don't you come with me?"

Rachel nodded and they headed for the woods behind the camp when Michelle stopped them. "Wait, why don't you let us help you?"

Alex believed she was trying to keep an eye on them. "There's no need. We can handle it. You two stay warm. You must be frozen."

He waited until Michelle sat back down before he and Rachel headed a little deeper into the woods and out of earshot.

"I don't know about the man, but she looks familiar. I only got a glimpse of the woman who showed up at my house this morning, but I think Michelle might be her. I recognize the voice." Rachel stepped closer, keeping her tone low. "She's armed, too. I'm sure he will be, as well. We need to get out of here as fast as possible. We don't know if they've called in backup yet."

Alex couldn't let go of the feeling that he knew Peter from somewhere. Was it just a coincidence that there were two bad guys who appeared familiar to him?

"You're right. There's no doubt that they know we're onto them. We'll have to find a way to neutralize the threat they pose." He glanced back at the couple by the fire.

"I have an idea. We said we were going for wood, so let's get some." She quickly gathered a few nearby sticks, as did Alex. "We should get back before they become too suspicious. Follow my lead and keep your weapon close."

Alex nodded and she drew in a breath and led the way back to the camp. As they neared, Alex could see the couple whispering to each other. They glanced back and saw them and broke apart guiltily.

"There you are. We were wondering if you two had decided to take off," Michelle said, and Alex attempted a smile.

"Now why would we do that?" While Alex didn't see a weapon, he suspected that they had them close by, which wouldn't leave him and Rachel much time to disarm them. He sure hoped her plan worked.

He watched as Rachel dropped her logs close to the fire. Alex placed a couple of sticks on the blaze itself, waiting for Rachel's cue. She held the final log in her hand and moved around the fire, pretending to stir it. She was now closest to Peter.

Without warning, she swung the log hard and hit Peter across the face. He keeled over backward, out cold.

Right away, Michelle searched beneath her sleeping bag, no doubt for a gun.

"I wouldn't if I were you." Rachel drew down

on Michelle, her voice reminding him of when they'd worked missions together.

With Rachel standing guard, Alex went over to the woman and grabbed the weapon she'd hidden, then checked under Peter's sleeping bag. There was a second gun.

"We were just worried for our safety. You guys were acting strangely," Michelle said, trying to convince them.

Alex ignored what she said and snatched up both backpacks. "We need to tie them up," he told Rachel. "I'll see if I can find some rope and secure him first."

Rachel kept the gun trained on Michelle's head. "Don't try anything foolish," she warned. "Or I promise you'll regret it."

Peter had just begun to regain consciousness when Alex retrieved some rope from one of the bags and forced Peter's hands behind his back, then secured them.

The minute Peter realized what was happening he fought against his restraints and raged. "How'd you let this happen?" He glared at Michelle and the woman actually shrunk away from the animosity on the man's face.

"That's enough," Alex ordered, and then moved to the woman. Once he'd tied up Michelle, he did a thorough search of both backpacks. What he found in one of them scared the daylights out of him. A phone. He brought up the number. It was the same phone that Liam had called him from. They had Liam's phone. What had they done with his friend?

FOUR

Across the burning fire, the look on Alex's face was alarming. He held Peter's backpack in his hand. Something was wrong. What had he found inside?

Please, don't let it be bad...

She held her breath. Their gazes locked and he silently tried to communicate something. He dropped the backpack and came over to where she stood, every step bringing more turbulence to her pulse.

"What is it?" She managed a whisper. The thought of losing her brother was terrifying.

Alex still held something in his hand. He silently motioned for them to step a little ways from the camp.

When they were out of earshot, he showed her a cell phone. She didn't recognize it. She shook her head. She didn't understand.

"I checked the number." His tone was tense, so

unlike Alex. Rachel braced for bad news. "This is the same phone Liam called me from before."

She stared at him as the implication of those words finally dawned. "Why would they have Liam's burner phone if they didn't know where he was?" When Alex had no answer, without thinking, Rachel charged back to Michelle and yanked her to her feet. "Where is he? What have you done with him?"

Taken aback, Michelle stared at her with fear in her eyes, struggling to get away. "I don't know who you're talking about. Let me go."

"You'd better keep your mouth shut." Peter glared over at his partner. Michelle visibly flinched. She was clearly terrified of Peter.

Alex went over to the man. "You're in no position to try to intimidate her. If you want to help yourself, you'd better start cooperating."

Peter wasn't swayed. "I have nothing to say." He shot Michelle a venomous look. "And neither does she."

"She can speak for herself." Alex took Michelle by the arm and pulled her away from Peter's hearing.

"Don't try anything foolish while we're gone," Rachel warned, and then followed Alex.

"He can't hurt you anymore," Alex told her. "We'll protect you, but you have to tell us what's going on here. Who are you working for? Where's Agent Carlson?" Michelle's brittle laugh cut through what he'd said.

"You have no idea what you're talking about," Michelle said in a hushed tone. She was visibly shaken and immediately seemed to regret her outburst. "My husband and I told you who we are. We came to you because we were lost and needed help, but you two have all but taken us hostage and we've done nothing wrong."

Alex held up the phone. "And this? I found it in Peter's backpack. It belongs to a friend of mine who's gone missing up here. A federal agent. How did you end up with his phone?"

Michelle glanced back at Peter and then looked Alex in the eye. "I don't know what you're talking about. You two are the first people we've run into. Maybe there are others here. People with bad intentions aimed toward your friend…and you."

Rachel sucked in a breath. "What do you mean by that?" She was convinced Michelle was trying to tell them they weren't alone up here. Or was she simply trying to dodge the question?

Michelle turned back toward Peter. "I have nothing else to say to you. And I would suggest you get out of here before you find yourself facing far worse trouble than you've seen so far."

Shocked, Rachel riveted her gaze to Alex.

There was no doubt in her mind the woman was trying her best to warn them without giving away too much.

Alex took Michelle back to where Peter was silently fuming. Then he motioned to Rachel and they stepped out of earshot once more.

"We need to get out of here now, Alex. I don't know what her intentions were for saying what she did, but I believe she was warning us there are others up here, searching for Liam and probably for us, as well."

Alex nodded then glanced over her shoulder to where the two sat. Michelle still looked afraid. Peter appeared to be browbeating her. "I think you're right. Their driver's licenses seem to back up their claim of who they are, but they could have been forged. And I'm positive I know this guy Peter from somewhere."

This bit of news was unsettling. He'd said the same about the man who had attacked them earlier. Did Alex recognize the men because they were part of the same organization as he was? It was an uneasy thought.

"Do you have any idea how?" It was too big of a coincidence that Alex would know two of the men that were hunting them down. They really needed to figure out why they were being chased so aggressively. Perhaps in the process it would lead to answers into Liam's location.

He shook his head, obviously frustrated by the elusive recollection. "I wish I knew. It's on the edge of my memory, but I just can't bring it out. Anyway, you're right. If what Michelle alluded to is correct, they could have men on the way here right now."

Which meant their window of escape was rapidly closing.

"What do we do about those two? We can't leave them up here in the elements."

"We stoke the fire and get out of here as quickly as possible before the people they've called catch up with us. Make no mistake—they didn't just happen upon us."

He was right. They'd probably been stalking them for a while.

"You need to let us go now." Peter talked in an overly loud voice once they'd returned to camp. Was he trying to alert his comrades to their location? "You can't leave us here. We'll freeze to death."

Alex ignored the man's raging and piled enough wood on the fire to last until morning.

"That should get you through the night. I'll be calling the authorities to let them know where they can pick you two up as soon as possible. I would suggest you tell them the truth."

"You can't leave us here," Michelle pleaded with Rachel. She could almost swear there was real fear in Michelle's eyes. Was it just an act? She'd had her chance to talk and had refused.

"You'll be fine until the authorities arrive," Rachel assured her. "The fire will keep any predators away."

Alex gathered up their phones and camping supplies. Rachel slipped on her backpack and they headed out in the opposite direction from where they believed Liam's meet had happened, trying to throw the two off as to where they were really heading.

Once they'd gone some distance from the campsite, Alex slowed down. "How are you holding up?" he asked.

Rachel glanced up at the sky filled with stars. "Okay, I guess. But I hate trying to make our way up to the top of Midnight Mountain at night." She thought about Michelle's warning. "I don't doubt for a second that Michelle was warning us there are more people up here searching for Liam and us. They probably called them to let them know they'd found us before they came into the camp."

Alex nodded. "I can't figure out her motives. She seemed genuinely scared, but when given the opportunity, she chose to back Peter. It could all be an act. Right now, we can't afford to trust her."

Rachel placed her hand on his arm and he

turned to look down at her. "We can't really call in the authorities, Alex. We don't know who's really behind Liam's disappearance. You saw the note Liam left. It's too dangerous."

Alex looked around the area uneasily. "I know. There's no doubt in my mind that there are others out there. I think Peter was trying to warn them of our exact location by talking loudly."

She'd thought the same thing. "We should be far enough away by now to circle back in the right direction."

They started off in the different path that would take them up to the top of the mountain. "It's getting colder by the minute." Alex turned the collar of his jacket up.

He was right. It felt as if the temperature had dropped at least ten degrees. Rachel rubbed her gloved hands together. "We need to keep walking just to stay warm."

The rugged mountain terrain made it impossible to keep up a good pace. Not to mention that they were traveling in the dark, unable to use flashlights to illuminate their way. They'd be sitting ducks if they were to happen upon the enemy.

Rachel's thoughts churned out questions by the dozens. The fact that Peter had Liam's phone wasn't a good thing. "How do you think they ended up with Liam's phone? There's no way they just happened upon it."

Alex stopped and faced her. In the darkness, she couldn't make out his expression. "No. They had him at one time. The fact that they're still searching for him gives me hope that Liam managed to get away. My gut is telling me he's still up here somewhere, though. The only question is, where? There's a lot of territory to cover and we have no clue as to where he might be hiding."

Rachel tried to hold on to some small amount of faith that Liam was still alive. She couldn't imagine her life without him. She searched her memory, going over every conversation she and Liam had had recently for anything that would give them a clue as to where he might be. She recalled something that Liam had told her once about one of his buddies from high school buying one of the logging camps up on the mountain. Was it possible that Liam had made it down to that area and was hiding there?

Please, Lord…

Alex was a few steps in front of her. Before she could tell him about what she'd remembered, he stopped dead in his tracks, putting his arm out in front of her to keep her from going any farther.

He turned back to her and whispered, "Voices."

Then he placed a finger over his lips. She heard it, too. The voices were coming from some distance ahead of them.

Alex pointed to a group of trees close by and they eased that way as quietly as possible.

Rachel tripped over a log, her foot rolled sideways, and she froze. But it was too late. The noise it made echoed throughout the still night.

"I hear something." A man's voice reached them. In the moonlight Rachel caught a glimpse of four people moving through the woods just a little ways from where they'd been walking.

She held her breath, praying that they hadn't been spotted. She and Alex were trained agents, but it was dark out and they were outnumbered.

Rachel tucked behind the closest tree, a pine that was barely large enough to conceal her from view. Alex had reached the group of trees he'd pointed to. Her gaze glued to his. Her heart pounded in her ears, drowning out all sound.

A flashlight's beam shot past the area where they were and Rachel sucked in her breath.

Please don't let them see us.

"There's nothing out there but a bunch of animals." A different voice than before snapped the words out. The flashlight hovered close to where Rachel was hiding. She tried to keep as still as possible. If she moved an inch, she'd be in the light. "They're waiting for us."

The man with the flashlight didn't make a move to obey. "I heard something." He kept the beam focused on the tree close to her for a second longer.

"And I'm telling you there's nothing there. He's waiting on us. You know how angry he gets when someone doesn't follow orders."

After what felt like an eternity, the man finally gave in. "Yeah, yeah, I'm coming." The light searched the area one more time and then she could hear them heading away. The same direction she and Alex had come.

Thank You, Lord, she whispered and struggled for a calm her heart wouldn't allow.

Once the men were safely out of the area, Rachel pointed up ahead. They needed to put as much space as they could between themselves and the men. When they reached Peter and Michelle, they'd know something was wrong. They'd put two and two together and realize the man had been right when he thought he heard something.

After she and Alex had covered more than a quarter of a mile, Rachel stopped for breath. "That was close. They're heading right toward where we left Peter and Michelle, as if they know exactly where to find them."

"I'm sure they do." Alex confirmed her belief. "I'll guarantee they called them in before they came out of the woods and confronted us. It won't take them long to reach those two and when they do, they'll come after us. We need to get out of sight as quickly as possible."

Once her heart finally stopped racing, Rachel remembered what she was going to tell Alex before they'd spotted the men.

"With everything that just happened, there wasn't time to tell you before. I remembered something Liam said to me not too long ago. I don't know why I didn't think of it earlier." She told him about Liam's friend buying one of the old mills.

"Do you remember which one? That could be where Liam is hiding out," he said in relief.

There were numerous logging camps up the mountain. Most were being reclaimed by the woods in which they were carved.

"There are several. We'll have to search them all." Not exactly the ideal situation, but they couldn't risk overlooking any of them on the off chance that Liam might be hiding there.

"Do you think you can find them in the dark?" Alex couldn't hide his doubt. He could barely see more than a couple of feet in front of him. Finding a bunch of deserted logging camps seemed like an impossible task in his mind.

"I think so, but I'm going to need the flashlight. We can't risk walking off the side of the mountain." She didn't sound nearly as positive as he had hoped.

"Lead the way," he told her, and she clicked on the flashlight and headed out.

While they walked, Alex couldn't shake the impression that he knew Peter from somewhere. He just couldn't pull the answer out of his head. That he seemed to recognize two bad men in one day told him he was onto something.

Rachel stopped to gain her bearings and he stood next to her. She brushed hair from her face. Even exhausted to the bone, she was beautiful. And every time he looked at her, he was dogged with regret. He'd messed things up between them. He'd been foolish enough to think that life revolved around the job. He'd been so wrong.

Thanks be to God, for working on Alex to help him see what was truly important. Still, it was a bitter pill to swallow that it had come at the expense of his relationship with Rachel.

"This way." She pointed a little farther up. "I remember Liam telling me once that his buddy hiked up here a lot before buying the place. He said it was one of the few camps on this side of the mountain."

They headed in that general direction, his thoughts keeping him quiet. Alex realized that he knew so little about her life now. Was she happy? Did she have regrets?

"Do you still hike the mountain?" he asked, mostly because he wanted to know more about her and he didn't want to bring up their touchy past.

Her steps faltered a little at the question. "Sometimes. Not as often as I'd like." She shrugged. "I feel so free up here. It's as if all the world's cares just melt away and it's just me alone up here with God."

He looked at her in surprise. Growing up, none of them had really been religious. He recalled attending church only at the big holidays. He hadn't paid much attention back then. He mostly just wanted the time he spent in church to be over. Yet everything had changed when he lost Rachel. He'd hit rock bottom for a while, doubting everything in his life. It was why he'd chosen to make a career change. He'd been searching for something different. Something more meaningful.

Joining the Scorpions, he'd found a tight-knit family where he belonged. Each member openly discussed their faith in God. He'd fought against the tugging at his heart for a bit, but the moment he gave in and realized he needed God in his life more than ever, the peace he felt inside at that decision was amazing.

He'd started attending a local church near their headquarters, and had grown closer to God ever since.

"I know what you mean," he told her quietly. "That's kind of how I feel when I hike the mountain near our compound. It's as if you can see God in everything."

She looked at him curiously. "Liam told me you'd joined a different branch of the CIA after I left. He said you seemed different. More at peace."

It surprised him to hear that Liam had noticed the change in him. "I guess I am." He didn't look at her. "Before, well, the job was everything to me. I couldn't imagine life without it." He shook his head and realized he had her full attention.

"What happened to change that?" She seemed genuinely interested in his answer.

"God happened," he said, and grinned over at her. "This new team that I joined, well, everyone there is a Christian, and they believe the work we are doing is God's work. When I joined, I was skeptical at first. You know I wasn't raised as a Christian. Back when we were kids, attending church felt like a chore, so I did it as seldom as possible."

He chuckled. "But then I realized these people were sincere. Soon, I started attending the church close to town and then I knew what was missing from my life. Now, I can't imagine where I'd be right now if I hadn't found the team."

She smiled up at him. "I get that. I was pretty messed up when I came home. Then I met Tom and Jenny and started attending church with them." She stopped for a second and he realized there was something more than she'd told him. "If it hadn't been for God, I'm not sure where I'd be right now."

Guilt tugged at his heartstrings. He didn't doubt for a moment that most of the reason why she'd been heading for trouble was because of him.

That he'd hurt her was painful to accept. It was hard letting go of their burdened past, but he did. She had married someone who could give her the things she'd needed. Things he couldn't. Best to leave that door closed.

His thoughts went back to the two men he seemingly recognized. They both appeared to be highly skilled. He had no doubt they possessed military training of some sort. How were they connected to Liam's disappearance and, more important, why did both men seem so familiar?

He considered what Rachel had said about Liam believing the person he'd been chasing might be CIA. Was that how Alex knew them? Had he run into the men as part of his job?

Alex pictured the two men in his head again. He focused on each one's facial features. It was on the tip of his tongue, just out of reach…and then it finally hit him why they both seemed familiar. He stopped dead in his tracks, drawing Rachel's worried attention back to him.

"What's wrong?" she asked.

Was it possible? He couldn't even believe it. His mind didn't want to go there.

He took a deep breath and voiced his fears aloud. "I told you that I thought I recognized Peter and the other man, Victor McNamara, who attacked us?" She nodded, her gaze plastered on his face.

"Well, I just remembered from where." He blew out a breath and shook his head.

Rachel saw how concerned he was. "How do you know them?" she prompted when he didn't answer right away.

"From CIA headquarters in Langley, Virginia." He tried to get the realization to make sense to him. It was absurd, surely.

"Langley?" She was clearly confused. "I don't remember either of them being at Langley."

He shook his head. "That's because we didn't train with them." He stopped and clasped her shoulders, needing a moment to fit it together in his head. "Rachel, those men are honored on the CIA's memorial wall. They're supposed to be dead. They were killed while on a mission a few years back. They aren't supposed to be alive anymore."

FIVE

Rachel stared up at him, trying to make sense of what Alex had just told her. "Why would they fake their deaths?" It was unimaginable.

He shook his head and they continued walking. "I can't imagine. I don't remember much of the details, only that their entire six-man team was killed while on a mission in Iraq. Peter Mullins and Victor McNamara are not their real names, though."

"Do you think they faked their deaths as part of their cover? Maybe they're still on a mission? They could be deep undercover with some really bad guys?" Even as she said the words aloud, the idea didn't make sense.

Alex shook his head. "No way. If they're up here chasing some bad guys, why are they trying to kill us and Liam?"

What Tom had told them earlier about Liam doing something bad chased through her thoughts, wholly unwelcomed. There was no way she would ever accept that her brother had gone rogue. Yet she couldn't dismiss what Alex had said about the men supposedly dying while on a mission in Iraq. That was the last place Liam had gone overseas. It couldn't simply be a coincidence.

Try as she might, Rachel couldn't seem to fit the pieces together. Exhaustion wasn't helping. She hadn't slept properly in days; she'd been too worried about her brother. She glanced around the wooded area. The first logging camp was still a good distance away. What would they do if those men had been there? Maybe they'd found Liam already? Would they be wasting precious time by searching the logging camps instead of going straight to Liam's last known location? If her brother were up there injured, he could be dead by the time they reached him. Her thoughts swam.

"Alex, what if he's still up there on the mountain somewhere, hurt and alone? Maybe we should keep heading up?"

He shook his head. "I don't think he's still up there, Rachel. Think about it. It's been over a week since we believe he went missing. These people have been searching up there all this time and I don't doubt for a minute that they knew about the meet location. If Liam were still up there, they would have found him by now."

Unless he were dead… She couldn't voice her deepest fear aloud. It didn't matter. Alex saw what she was thinking.

"Don't go there. If Liam were truly dead, they wouldn't still be up here. They'd have what they wanted and they'd be long gone. He's still alive and he has the advantage. Liam knows this place like the back of his hand. All of the mountain's secret hiding places. These men do not. Liam would know where to go to disappear until it was safe to leave."

Rachel hung on to that promise with everything inside of her. Alex was right. Liam could find every cave up on the mountainside in the dark. If her brother were injured, it would slow him down. Depending on how serious his injuries might be, it was possible he couldn't leave by his own strength.

"How much farther to the first camp?" Alex asked while keeping a careful eye behind them. "Those men must have reached Peter and Michelle by now. They can't let us go because they believe Liam may have told you something critical that they don't want made public."

The implication was frightening. These men were willing to kill to keep their secret.

Exhausted and barely hanging on, she and Alex didn't have the luxury of taking a break.

"It's still a little ways from here." She hated

telling him the next part, but he needed to know. "Alex, there's some pretty rough terrain standing between us and the camp. The loggers used to reach the camp by coming up from the opposite side of the mountain where it's more accessible."

"What's standing between us and the camp?" he asked, as if dreading her answer.

It had been a while since Rachel visited the area, but if she remembered correctly, there was a creek that ran through here. It fed off the spring thaws and it would be raging at this time of the year.

"Water," she answered. "There's a creek a couple of miles before we reach the camp. We had a lot of snow this year. It's going to be running pretty swiftly."

She could see this wasn't exactly the best news. "Let's hope it's still pretty frozen up here. Otherwise, we're going to get wet, and with the temperature close to freezing, we could be in serious danger of hypothermia."

Alex felt the exhaustion of the day seep into his limbs. He was working on next to no sleep. He couldn't imagine what Rachel was going through.

"The creek is just past this next ridge." He glanced at her. She was shivering from the cold.

They wouldn't be any good to Liam or anyone else if they died up here from the elements.

Rachel stopped suddenly and listened. "I hear it." She turned to him. "We're almost there, Alex. It sounds like it's running pretty strong."

Crossing a fast-moving creek would be next to impossible under the best of conditions. In the dark and ill prepared for the crossing, it might cost them both their lives.

They reached the top of the summit. Alex could see the white water rushing below them. It appeared as if the creek had overflown its banks. The worst possible scenario. His heart sank. "Maybe there's an easier way to cross. We have to try."

He and Rachel made their way slowly to the edge. At one time the water had been much higher. There was evidence of flooding all around them. Alex's feet slogged through thick mud as they neared the edge of the water.

He stopped once they got as close as the rushing water would allow. There were charred trees all around. Not too long ago, there had been a fire up here, no doubt from a lightning strike. It happened frequently in the mountains. The fire had taken out most of the trees in a wide swatch on either side of the creek bank. Only a couple of trees still stood and they were as charred ghosts tottering on the edge of the bank.

As he surveyed the opposite bank, Alex had an idea. "There's still some rope in one of the backpacks. If we can lasso that tree across the creek then tie onto this one here, I think we can make it across the water."

It was a long shot, but it was their only option. They couldn't stay here until morning, and to try to find another way around the creek would cost them precious time.

"How are your lassoing skills?" Rachel asked with a weary smile. Even though she was exhausted and travel worn, looking at her still had the power to make his pulse race. He'd do just about anything in his power, lay down his life if need be, to protect her.

"Rusty, but I think I can manage. I'll need some light, though."

She shone the flashlight his way in response.

"Thanks. I know it's risky, but otherwise we could be here for a while."

She followed him over to the edge of the creek. Rachel shone the light across the creek to where a single tree had survived the fire.

It was a long shot at best. *Lord, I need Your help*, Alex prayed.

"I think I can hook it around that branch up there. It's tall enough to keep us out of the water, at least."

Rachel took out the rope and handed it to Alex.

As a kid, Alex had loved to rope just about anything in sight. He'd given up on becoming a professional bull roper when his interests turned to other things as a teen...mostly Rachel.

Holding the greater portion of the rope in his left hand, Alex swung the lariat above his head. It took five tries, three more than it should have in the old days, to lasso the branch in question.

"You haven't lost your touch." Rachel smiled brightly. "And I'm sure glad you haven't."

He jerked the rope tight and tested the branch for stability. Having survived the fire, it could be compromised, but they were all out of choices. It was this or turn around and head back the way they'd come and risk running into those men.

"It looks like it should hold our weight. We just need to tie it off on this end." The remaining tree on their side of the bank wasn't nearly as sturdy looking.

"Let's hope it holds up," she said and shone the light on the charred tree. She was right. If the tree fell, they could be in serious trouble. If they landed in that water, they'd be swept downstream before they had a chance to save themselves.

Alex looped the rope around the tree and started tying it off. Before he'd finished, he heard voices coming from just over the ridge.

Rachel glanced behind them. "Alex, they're

almost here. We have to hurry." He took her hand and they headed to the edge of the creek.

"You should go ahead of me. I'm positive it will hold your weight. I'm not sure about mine. If they reach me before I can cross, cut the rope and get out of here. Find Liam."

He didn't get to finish before she shook her head. "I'm not leaving you behind. We're in this together."

His gaze clung to hers. So many unspoken feelings weighed on his mind. He had to protect her.

"Rachel, I..." He wasn't sure what he wanted to tell her, only that he needed her to understand that he still cared about her.

She placed her finger over his lips. "No, you're going to make it and I'm not leaving this area without you. We're going to find Liam and this is all going to be a bad memory someday."

He knew it would be pointless to argue. Time was precious. While the voices still sounded a little ways away, it wouldn't take them long to reach the creek. Crossing the water by rope was going to be time-consuming.

She tucked her weapon behind her back. Alex gave her a boost up to the rope. Rachel put one hand in front of the other, slowly pulling her way across past the bank and over the raging water. The process was excruciatingly slow. The creek wouldn't normally be as wide to cross, but with the additional water running, it had doubled in capacity.

Behind him, multiple voices grew nearer. Rachel was barely midway across the creek. He didn't dare start across until she was safely on the opposite bank. With his weight, it could snap one of the tree branches and they'd both land in the freezing water.

Keeping a careful eye on Rachel's progress, Alex glanced behind him. He could see several flashlight beams bouncing across the night sky.

Hurry, Rachel…

She was almost to the other bank. Like it or not, he had to start making his way across.

With his gloves on, Alex jumped as high as he could and managed to grasp the rope. Working as quickly as he could, he placed one hand in front of the other until he was over the water. He heard the tree make a cracking, groaning noise. Was it about to snap?

On the ground now, Rachel watched him make his way over the water. "Hurry, Alex. They're coming down the ridge now." She took out her Glock and fired on the advancing men while Alex did his best to double his speed. He was still a little ways from the bank when the men returned Rachel's shots. He was caught in the cross fire. One stray bullet and he was dead.

With a couple of feet still left between him and the bank, Alex took out his knife. While balancing with one hand, he cut the rope behind him. Immediately, he plunged toward the creek. Alex jumped with all his strength toward the bank's edge, barely hitting it. Then he tucked and rolled.

"Let's get out of here," he said the second he was on his feet again. Together they kept low to the ground as bullets continued to whiz past their heads.

"Get some rope," one of the men behind them yelled. "If they can cross that way, we can, too."

"We can't let them get across," Rachel said as she continued firing at the enemy.

With his thoughts struggling to find a solution, only one came to mind. He'd need to find a way to pull the tree over. He remembered there was a small ax among the camping supplies.

"This is the only tree for them to tie to on this side of the bank. If I can get it down, they won't be able to cross." Like it or not, it was their only chance to stay alive.

SIX

Rachel glanced back at the tree. "You'll be exposed. They have nothing to lose. And I hate to point this out, but even with using the weapons we took from Peter and Michelle, we don't have an unlimited amount of ammo."

They had both brought extra clips of bullets and had the confiscated weapons, but if they had to continue to defend themselves like this, their supply wouldn't hold out long.

His gaze held hers. "It's our only choice. I'll be okay."

She slowly nodded. "Okay, I've got your back. Do what you have to do."

Alex grabbed the small ax from the backpack and slowly edged his way over to the tree in question. He had barely left the area where they were hiding before the men spotted the movement and began firing right away.

From her vantage point, Rachel engaged the men. She glanced back over her shoulder. Alex had reached the tree and was on the backside, as out of sight as possible. Because the ax was so small, she knew it would take longer to bring the tree down.

As she continued to return fire, she saw the tree give way ever so slightly out of the corner of her eye.

While the men continued shooting, she felt the blowback from bullets close by. She couldn't hold them off for long.

"Hurry, Alex." Time was running out. She watched him gather his strength, and with one final swing of the ax, the tree came crashing down, barely missing him.

He hurried back to her. "That should buy us some time. We need to make it to those woods over there. Go ahead of me. I'll cover you."

She ducked low and ran for the woods while Alex continued to fire at the men. Once she'd reached the trees, he charged for the woods while Rachel covered him.

"Let's get out of here," he said. "I have no doubt that they'll find another way across soon enough."

They hurried into the wilderness. Rachel glanced back briefly. The men were slowly coming out of their hiding places. How long before they crossed the creek?

After they had covered more than a quarter of

a mile through dense foliage, the woods begin to thin out slightly.

"We must be close to the camp. We need to search this area quickly. If Liam's here, we won't have long to find him and get out of here."

Alex nodded. "Let's just hope this is the right camp."

Rachel stopped once they reached the edge. "What if he's not here?"

"Then we keep looking. Let's take a quick look around the place and see if there's any sign of him."

Working as fast as they possibly could, they searched the crumbling camp, but Liam wasn't there.

Rachel couldn't have been more discouraged. "This can't be the camp Liam mentioned."

Alex touched her cheek. "We can't give up. You said yourself there are several other camps up here. We just need to find the right one."

She nodded. Alex was right. She had to keep fighting for Liam. She struggled to recall the particular layout on this side of the mountain. "The next one should be a little ways up the mountain from here."

"Good. Let's keep going. Perhaps, if those guys come this way, they'll think we kept heading downhill. How are you holding up?" Alex asked when she stumbled slightly.

"Tired, but I'm okay. Don't worry, I can keep up." She wished she felt more confident. She wasn't used to this kind of pace.

"Let's stop and rest for a moment." He pointed to a fallen tree and she sat down. Alex took out one of the water bottles and handed it to her.

"Thanks." She took it gratefully and drank deeply.

Alex looked around the desolate area. "It doesn't look as if anyone's been up here in a long time."

He was probably right. The camp they'd just left was overgrown; the woods had reclaimed most of its remaining buildings.

"Liam said that's why his friend wanted to buy the camp he did. It hadn't been used in years, so he got a good price. He wanted to make the camp a working lumber mill again."

She handed Alex the water and he took a drink, then put the bottle back in his backpack.

"There's certainly enough timber up here to run several mills, especially if it's been years since the area has been harvested." He blew out a sigh. "As much as I hate to say it, we need to move on. We don't know if they've found their way across the creek yet."

As they headed deeper into the woods, getting into the higher altitude forced them to slow their steps down tremendously.

Rachel found herself listening to every little noise around them. She'd been in the woods since she was a kid, but this was different. She'd never been chased by people intent on taking her life.

As she had so many times since Liam's disappearance, Rachel thought about her brother's last visit. Liam had alluded to the fact that someone from the CIA might be involved with the terrorist threat he'd been chasing. His comment on the map he left seemed to indicate he believed it, and now there were presumed CIA agents combing the area looking for Liam. All things pointed to the same conclusion Liam had come to.

What if these men were somehow working for the same terrorist that Liam had been chasing? She voiced her concerns aloud. "If Liam discovered the connection, he could pose a threat to any further attacks."

Alex's expression was grim. "What are they doing here in the US? There's no way they'd travel all this way just to track down Liam because of something he knows. They'd risk blowing their cover. There's something more going on."

A disturbing thought dawned on her. "Unless Liam has something they want."

Alex stopped and stared at her. "What would

be worth coming out of hiding and risking their lives for?"

Rachel shook her head. "I don't know. Whatever it is, it must be big."

"Let's just hope we find Liam at the next camp. We need answers, Rachel, before this thing escalates any further."

It felt as if they'd been hiking for hours and they still hadn't come across the camp. So far, there was no sign of the men, but she didn't doubt they would have found a way to cross the creek. They weren't about to give up, especially if what she suspected were true and Liam had taken something important from them.

As she walked, she kept going back over what had happened. One thing bothered her. "Did you see Michelle or Peter back there?" Where were they?

Alex shook his head. "No. I have no idea where they are. Right now, you're the only connection they have with Liam, so why not put every man available into capturing us?"

"Unless they're searching for something else... Maybe whatever Liam took."

He stopped dead in his tracks. The dawning of what she'd just said registered an alarm. "You think?"

"Somewhere here in the US could be their next target. What if they planned to attack someplace here and Liam discovered it? Liam tracked them here, found whatever they brought in to do the attack with, and hid it somewhere up here. They would be desperate to get it back. They have nothing to lose."

If what Rachel said were true, then this thing was much bigger than either of them had originally believed. They needed help.

"Rachel, we're in way over our heads. Let me reach out to my commander for backup." When she didn't answer he pressed. "We're outnumbered and certainly outgunned. Our ammo supply won't last past another confrontation. We have no idea how many more men these guys have up here searching for Liam and whatever else they're looking for. We could die." He hated pointing out the obvious, but the truth had to be faced.

He could see from her mutinous expression that she wasn't ready to give in. "We can't. You said yourself these men are CIA. We don't know how deep their connections go. Even if your people aren't involved, they could still inadvertently tip off someone who is. We can't risk it now. Liam's life is on the line."

Her answer didn't surprise him and he certainly couldn't blame her, but he had a feeling at some point they'd have no other choice but to reach out to Jase and the Scorpion team for help. He just hoped he could convince her to do so before it was too late.

Rachel took out the binoculars and activated the night-vision function, homing in on something off in the distance.

"Do you see something?" he asked.

"Yes, just up ahead. I think it's the second camp." She handed him the binoculars.

From what he could tell so far, nothing about the second camp was reassuring. It appeared as overgrown as the last one. Alex chose to keep his misgivings to himself. "Let's hope we find Liam there. Then we can get out of here and figure out what's really going on."

The exhaustion of the hike had begun to take its toll on his body. His legs felt like rubber. He was fit and used to the rigor. He couldn't imagine how Rachel was feeling.

Once they reached the opening leading into the camp, Alex stopped to take in their surroundings. In the dark, it was hard to tell much about the place, only that it appeared as if it had been years since anyone had been there. The surrounding woods had already reclaimed parts of the camp. But then Rachel had said that was one of the reasons Liam's friend had wanted to buy the place.

"We can't afford to use the flashlight. We

could be walking into a trap." The hackles along his neck stood at attention. He didn't like it. "Maybe you should wait here. Let me check it out first."

He didn't have to look at her to see her reaction. "As I told you before, Alex, we're in this together, I'm coming with you."

He touched her face gently. Losing her again was an unbearable thought, but he knew it was useless to argue.

Please keep us safe…

"Ready?" he asked, the weight of what he wanted to tell her roughening his voice.

She covered his hand. "Yes, I'm ready."

Alex shoved branches away and stepped into what had once been a camp.

When they were in the clearing, he stopped for a moment to listen. Only the sounds of the night could be heard around them. Still, the uneasiness in the pit of his stomach had him on full alert.

"Let's start over there." He leaned in close and whispered so that only she could hear. The last thing they needed was to alert anyone with deadly intent. He pointed to a particular area. "There's a couple of buildings still standing. He could be in one of them. Stay close. I don't like this."

Alex could see the uneasiness he felt reflected

in her eyes as they slowly advanced into the camp. The first building they came upon had collapsed in upon itself. It appeared to be where the trees were milled at one time.

"I can't see anything on the inside." He took out his flashlight and shone it around the dilapidated building. "There's nothing here."

An unsettling thought occurred. What if the camp were empty? They'd have no choice but to keep climbing up the mountain to Liam's last known location. By coming this way, they'd cost themselves several hours of valuable time. If Liam were injured, it could mean the difference between life and death.

The next building appeared to be living quarters of some type, mostly intact. Alex stopped next to the door. It took several tries for it to free itself of years of decay.

Once it screeched open, he and Rachel eased inside. It took a few minutes for his eyes to become accustomed to the darkness enough to make out shapes.

The place consisted of a single room. What appeared to be a broken-down table was shoved into one corner. On the opposite wall a bed was set up. There was nothing else. Alex's heart sank. It didn't appear that anyone had been here in a while, either.

Frustrated, he turned back to Rachel. "It's

empty." He barely got the words out when a noise that sounded like a wounded animal came from the area where the bed was located.

"What was that?" Rachel asked.

Alex whirled around to survey the area. "I don't see anything." He slowly advanced to the bed with his weapon drawn. Had some animal gotten injured and crawled inside the cabin to seek refuge?

There was nothing but a ratty old mattress on top of the bed. He realized the noise was coming from under it.

He indicated that Rachel should cover him. Alex clicked on the flashlight and counted off three in his head. Then he grabbed the bed and shoved it out of the way.

Huddled beneath it was a badly injured man who had clearly been shot. But the most disturbing part was the fact that Alex recognized this man, too. He knew him. Had worked several missions with him. This was the legendary CIA agent Deacon Broderick.

SEVEN

Rachel tucked her weapon behind her back and hurried to the man's side. He seemed to be caught somewhere between consciousness and unconsciousness. It took only a cursory exam to realize he was in bad shape. "He's been shot in the shoulder and leg. He's lost a lot of blood."

Alex knelt next to her and undid the man's shirt. "Someone's bandaged the wounds," he said in amazement. "Still, he needs proper medical care right away."

"Do you know him?" Rachel asked. She'd seen the way Alex looked at the man.

He searched the man's pockets and come up empty. "Yes, I know him. I've worked with him before. His name is Deacon Broderick." His gaze slid to hers. "He's CIA, Rachel. And he's a legend at that. Deacon has helped take down some of the biggest threats around the world."

She couldn't believe it. If this man was CIA, then what was his connection to the supposed deceased agents? "Do you think he's working with the others?"

Alex shook his head. "No way. Deacon is a stand-up guy. He may know something about Liam's disappearance, though."

His attempt to rouse the man proved futile. Deacon continued to mumble incoherently. "He's delirious. We need to get him help."

Alex was right. It was time to reach out to the Scorpions for assistance. A man's life was in danger. Liam was still missing and they were way outmanned. "You should call your command. Tell them where we are so that they can send help. We can't let Deacon die."

Alex clutched her arm and smiled. She could see his relief. "I'll make the call. Can you try to keep him as comfortable as possible?"

"Go. I'll see what I can do to help Deacon."

While in the field, Rachel had gotten used to dealing with medical emergencies, especially gunshot wounds. She had no idea how long Deacon had been lying here injured, but there was little doubt in her mind that without further expert attention he wouldn't survive long.

She eased his shirt away from the wound to get a better look. Whoever had bandaged the wounds had done a good job. She glanced around for something to use as a bandage and noticed that there were extra strips of cloth matching the ones used. It looked like someone had ripped apart a flannel shirt to use. Next to the cloth, there was a half a dozen empty water bottles there, as well.

Rachel took it as a good sign that perhaps Deacon hadn't been this bad off when he'd reached the camp. She slowly eased the old bandage from the wound and examined it. Deacon moaned in pain. It appeared that the bullet had gone straight through. A good sign. It didn't look as if infection had set in yet. Once she'd cleaned the wound with the water, she wrapped it as tight as she could.

Alex returned and helped her with Deacon's leg injury. It was just a grazing shot and not nearly as bad.

Once they'd finished, she and Alex stepped away.

"Did you get in touch with your team?" she asked anxiously.

He shook his head. "The phone service is nonexistent here. I'll need to see if I can find a spot higher up. Maybe I can pick up a tower from there. Will you be okay by yourself for a bit?"

"Of course." She looked into his eyes and her breath caught at what she saw there.

He stepped closer, his voice rough with feeling. "Rachel…"

She believed she knew what he was going to say and she couldn't let him. It was best not to open that door again. She shook her head. "No, it's okay. You don't have to say it."

Regret reflected on his face and she turned away. She didn't want to hear his regrets.

The door closed quietly behind him. Rachel drew in a shaky breath. Her feelings for Alex had no place in the hunt for Liam. She had to keep her focus on finding her brother. And Deacon needed immediate medical attention.

She shoved her own regret down deep and went back to the man. He was perspiring and mumbling to himself, unaware of what was going on around him.

Rachel touched his arm and lifted up a prayer for his safekeeping.

Someone had obviously cared for Deacon's injuries. If it were the enemy, they would have left him wherever he was to die. Was it possible that Liam had done this? Her brother wore flannel shirts similar to those used as the bandages.

The sight of it gave her hope that her brother had brought Deacon here to keep him safe. Perhaps Liam had tried to hike out to get assistance. Did he have a cell phone with him? Deacon had nothing on him, including any form of ID.

She bunched some of the remaining strips of cloth under Deacon's head as a makeshift pillow, then got out the extra jacket she'd brought in her backpack and placed it over him for warmth.

One thing was for certain—they couldn't stay here long. Those men could show up at any moment and every second they were here meant Deacon's condition could worsen.

Lack of sleep and the physical strain of hiking the mountain had taken its toll. Not to mention the emotional roller-coaster ride she'd been on since Liam disappeared. Nothing made sense. Once they were on safer ground and they found Liam, maybe they could figure out who was behind this horror.

When Alex returned a few minutes later she hoped he had good news.

"I was able to reach my commander. He's dispatching several choppers right away, but we may not have that long." He had a worried look on his face. He nodded toward Deacon. "Rachel, we need to get Deacon out of here right away."

Alex was right. The man's life was on the line. "What do you suggest?" she asked.

"I saw an old logging truck out back. If I can get it running, we can head down the mountain to Hendersonville. There's still a hospital there, right? Let's hope these men won't be looking for us there. Then, once Jase and the team arrive, we can continue our search for Liam."

She knew it was the best plan to save Deacon's life, but the thought of abandoning Liam even for a little while tore at her conscience.

He seemed able to read all of her thoughts. "We're not leaving him up here. We are just saving Deacon."

She slowly nodded. "You're right. He needs our help the most."

Rachel could tell there was something else on his mind. "Did you find out something?"

He heaved a sigh that spoke volumes. "I did. I talked to Jase about the agents that were supposed to be dead. He remembered hearing the story behind the agents' deaths from another former Scorpion commander by the name of Kyle Jennings." Alex hesitated as if recalling the conversation. "Kyle told him that the men were in Iraq on a mission, searching for the Chemist, an elusive man who had perfected the recipe for sarin gas and was selling it on the dark web to the highest bidder. The team was spearheaded by a senior agent by the name of Blake Temple. Jase said Blake seemed to have an unusual interest in bringing down the Chemist. Kyle assumed he was just dedicated to the task at hand. I don't know if that's the case."

How did the missing agent's reappearance and the story of the Chemist fit into Liam's disappearance?

"Now I understand why Peter looked particu-

larly familiar to me. Rachel, he's Blake Temple."
He held her gaze. Saw the surprise she couldn't
hide. "If these men came out of hiding, it has to
be for something big."

He was right. There was no way they'd risk
being captured unless they were desperate. "I
wonder how Michelle fits into all of this."

"I have no idea. I couldn't get a good read off
her." He shook his head. "At least we have help
on the way. The sooner we get Deacon out of
here, the better, though. I'll go see if I can get
that truck running before Temple and the rest
of his thugs catch up with us."

He turned to leave, but she caught his arm.
She wasn't ready to answer the questions she
saw in his eyes just yet. "Please be careful," she
said in a whisper of a voice.

"I will." The hint of a smile was filled with
sadness. He'd expected more. She wished she
could give it to him. After she was alone, regret crawled into every fiber of her being. Alex
wasn't the same person he'd been earlier and
that was easy to see. But was there a chance for
them? She couldn't let herself go there. She'd
lost her heart to him once. She couldn't afford
to do so again.

Rachel checked on Deacon once more. He
seemed to be resting somewhat more comfort-
ably. It was still hours before daylight. If Alex

could get the truck running, they might be able to leave the area before sunrise, which would give them a better chance at escaping the men chasing them.

"Where are you, Liam?" she whispered into the cold air, but her only answer was the mutterings of the injured man close by.

Rachel went over to the window behind the cabin and glanced out at the darkness. She could see Alex's flashlight beam as he worked to bring the truck to life.

Where were the men? Had they actually bought their decoy? As much as she wanted to believe, she didn't. These men had survived for years without detection. They were highly trained agents just like she and Alex. They would think in the same way. They'd keep coming until they found them.

"Liam! Get down!" Deacon called out in a panic. Rachel whirled from the window. Deacon knew about her brother!

She was still trying to make sense of it when Alex came back inside.

"It won't make it far, but I think we can get down the mountain in it if we're careful..." He stopped when he got a good look at her shocked expression. "What happened?"

"Deacon just mentioned Liam by name." She

told him what Deacon had said. "Alex, what if Deacon is Liam's asset?"

Alex stared at the unconscious man. "I guess it's possible. But why was Deacon working with Liam?"

Rachel shook her head. "I wish I knew. Do you know what type of work Deacon was doing recently?" If Alex knew what he was working on, maybe they could figure out why Liam had asked to meet with Deacon.

"It's been a while since I worked with him. But I do know that Deacon was responsible for bringing down some major players in the terrorism game."

Maybe Deacon had information about the agents or the Chemist or… She had never felt so frustrated before. It was like trying to fit together a puzzle with half the pieces missing.

Alex came over to her and tipped her chin so that she looked into his eyes. "We'll never figure it out without Deacon's or Liam's help. But we *will* figure it out. Liam's a survivor. He's been in far worse circumstances than this."

She wanted to believe that. "If he brought Deacon down here, why wouldn't he hike out on foot to get help?"

Alex shook his head. "I don't know. But right now we need to concentrate on saving Deacon's life."

As worried as she was about Liam, Deacon needed their help immediately.

"I'll bring the truck around and then we can get him into the back seat where he can lie down."

Alex still held her, searching her face. She struggled to bring enough air into her lungs. With another intense look, he let her go and went to get the truck. She was grateful to be left alone because she so needed to control her racing pulse. Alex had a way of getting to her like no one else. She'd loved him so much. Part of her heart would always belong to him, but she needed to keep her focus on helping Deacon and saving Liam. If her thoughts wandered back to the past it wouldn't benefit anyone.

As hard as she tried, Rachel still couldn't settle in her mind why Liam had brought Deacon all the way here and then left him. Something must have forced Liam to leave in a hurry.

Before she could try to bring her chaotic thoughts together, the noise of gunfire coming from the woods nearby exploded all around. Rachel grabbed her weapon and hurried to the front of the cabin where the shots seemed to have originated. Her hand had barely touched the door handle when it flew open and Alex rushed inside and slammed the door closed.

The fear she saw in his eyes scared her. "What's happening out there?"

"They've found us. We have to get out before they surround the cabin and have us trapped inside…" He stopped for a second before adding, "I don't think it's wise to take Deacon with us under these conditions. The hectic pace would be too much for him."

They'd have to leave Deacon behind. But if those men found him here, they'd finish what they started and kill him.

Rachel hurried over to the injured man. "What should we do? What if they search the cabin? They'll kill him."

There was really only one option. "We'll cover him with the bed again. I have an extra jacket. Hopefully, between the two, he can stay warm enough until Jase's team arrives. If we can successfully lead them away from here, he should be safe enough."

Alex put his extra jacket over Deacon and tried to make him as comfortable as possible, then together they placed the bed over the top of him. Alex prayed that Deacon would be safe until help arrived. "We have to hurry, Rachel. They're not far."

They grabbed their gear and headed out to where Alex had left the old beat-up truck running.

Rachel slid in the driver's side and Alex followed. He shoved the truck in gear and turned the vehicle toward the rudimentary road that had been carved out of the woods.

"Hang on," he told her. "I'm afraid this is going to be one hairy ride."

He was right. Rachel clung to the door handle as the truck bounced over downed trees and debris left from years of logging. Alex kept his attention on the road ahead as it tested all his skills. Where were the men he'd spotted in the woods? He was pretty sure he'd hit one of them, but by his best account there had been at least half a dozen others up on the hill above the camp.

The headlights of the truck were so bad that he could barely see where they were going. He was forced to slow the truck's speed down to a crawl as he rounded a curve.

Ice still clung to the road in places where the sunlight didn't reach. The truck slid sideways and close to the mountain's edge. Rachel stifled a scream in response.

Somehow, Alex got the truck back on the path, but his hands shook from the close call. Doing his best to dodge downed trees, he continued to weave down the mountainside.

Without warning, the front windshield exploded. Both Alex and Rachel ducked as glass flew everywhere, narrowly missing their eyes.

Another round riddled the passenger side of the truck. Alex could barely see where he was going as the shots continued to ricochet off the truck, and he was forced to stay low. He managed a quick glance ahead and saw five men emerge in front of them, weapons aimed at the truck.

Alex slammed the brakes on hard. The men kept advancing. They were all out of options. If they continued forward, they'd be shot. Desperate to keep them alive, Alex shoved the vehicle in Reverse and tried to keep the truck on the trail.

"Get down." He barely got the words out when the men opened fire. Alex whipped the truck around and headed back the direction they'd come.

"We need to find another way out of here. Otherwise, we're trapped." Alex glanced over at Rachel. She was white as a sheet. "They're on foot. We're not," he said without feeling nearly as confident about what he'd said. He'd scouted the area briefly. This was the only road he'd seen. "Do you remember the layout of what's just below this camp?" The road in front of them quickly disappeared and was replaced with overgrown brush.

"Alex, there's no road past the camp. There's

nothing." She confirmed his worst fears. "We'll never make it down this way."

He barely had time to process what she said before he realized they were now surrounded by armed men. There would be no escaping now.

EIGHT

Alex hit the brakes as the men circled the truck.

Rachel watched the men advancing on them. "What do we do now?" she forced out.

She saw the reality of their situation reflected in his eyes. "We give up."

She couldn't believe what she heard. They were still no closer to knowing what had happened to Liam than when they'd first started. "No, Alex, we can't. We have to keep fighting."

He shook his head. "If we resist, we'll be dead. We have to stay alive. It's the only way to save Deacon and find Liam."

Tears filled her eyes. She knew he was right. She didn't want to die here. Not without knowing what had happened to her brother. Not with things still unsettled between herself and Alex.

"They wouldn't be coming after us this hard if they'd found Liam," Alex reasoned. "I believe they still need us. They won't kill us if we don't resist. Maybe we can buy enough time for my team to arrive."

As she looked at his handsome face, there were so many things she wanted to say, but now was not the time. She would fight with everything inside her to live another day because she wanted to have the chance to tell Alex everything that was in her heart.

With a smile of encouragement for her sake, Alex yelled, "Hold your fire. We're coming out." To her he said, "Do what I do, okay?"

He waited for her to confirm, then he slowly opened the driver's-side door. With his hands in the air, he got out. Rachel hesitated a second longer before doing the same.

"Search them," one of the men shouted, and someone jerked Alex forward and quickly patted him down. They took his gun and phone right away. Their backpacks with all their supplies were still in the truck.

Another man forced Rachel to turn around, then he searched her. Alex tried to free himself to get to her side, but his captor slugged him hard in the gut. He dropped to his knees. The man reached for him again.

"No, stop. Don't hurt him. We're cooperating with you." Rachel was terrified they'd kill Alex.

The person looming over Alex hauled him to his feet.

"Get them back to the cabin," said the man who had ordered his men to search them. She and Alex were forced into the bed of the truck, along with several armed men, and driven back to the cabin where they'd left Deacon. What they'd tried to prevent was happening.

Don't let them find Deacon.

The man holding Rachel's arm in a viselike grip shoved her hard, and she flew into the cabin, almost losing her balance.

Alex freed himself from his restrainer and hurried to her side. "Are you okay?" he asked while glaring at the man who'd shoved her.

"I'm fine." She touched his arm and forced his gaze to her. "I'm okay, Alex."

The anger slowly evaporated from him. They both needed to keep their wits about them if they stood any chance of surviving.

The leader stepped forward, inches from Rachel's face. With his arms crossed, he stared her down. "Well, we finally caught you two. I'll admit you gave us a good run. Just not good enough." His smile held no humor in it. Right away, Rachel recognized him. It was the former CIA agent Victor McNamara.

"Why were you trying to kill us?" Rachel demanded.

McNamara smirked. "If we were trying to kill you two, you'd be dead by now." McNamara's words seemed to confirm what Alex said earlier. These men had no idea where Liam was.

One of the men handed McNamara Alex's driver's license. He stared at it and then Alex while Rachel held on to her breath. If he recognized Alex as a CIA agent, no matter what he'd claimed earlier, he'd kill him.

"How do you fit into this?" McNamara demanded, but Alex kept silent. McNamara motioned to one of his thugs, who grabbed Alex and slugged him hard once more.

"Stop," Rachel cried out as Alex doubled over in pain. She tried to come to his aid, but someone grabbed her arms, holding her in place.

"I'll ask you again. How do you fit into Agent Carlson's crimes?"

Agent Carlson's crimes... The words settled over her.

"What are you talking about?" Rachel demanded. She wasn't about to let them sully Liam's name. "My brother hasn't committed any crimes."

McNamara turned his full attention on her. "Ah, the sister," he sneered. "You clearly have no idea who your brother really is." She had to struggle not to take the bait. "Your brother, along with Deacon Broderick, has stolen some very deadly weapons. My team and I have been searching for them for quite some time. We had them surrounded up on the mountain, but they both managed to give us the slip. Not without being wounded first, I might add. They won't get far on their own. I believe you know where your brother might be hiding. Why else would you be up here? For his own well-being, I suggest you tell me where, so that we can find him alive."

McNamara was talking as if he were still an agent. He had no idea they knew the truth.

"Tie them both up." He barked the order to one of his men, who grabbed Alex. Forcing his arms together, he wrapped the rope tight around his wrists. Another man did the same to Rachel, and she winced in pain.

"Who are you? Why should I tell you anything?" Rachel tried to hold on to her composure when McNamara stepped to within inches of her face.

"I'm the only person who can keep your brother from facing the death sentence for treason."

Treason. "How can *you* charge Liam with treason?" she exclaimed, astonished. She had to hear him say who he was.

"Because I'm working for the CIA and I've been trying to bring down a terrorist known as the Chemist for a long time. Turns out, your brother knew him all along. They've been smuggling large amounts of sarin gas into the States together. Who knows to what deadly purpose?"

She couldn't afford to give anything away. "That's a lie. My brother did nothing of the sort."

McNamara's smile sent a shiver down her back. "You really don't know how deeply involved in this thing your brother really is." She raised her chin, refusing to give in to his bluff.

With a shake of his head, McNamara went back over to his men. He said something to them that she couldn't discern. She had the impression that they were waiting on something...or someone.

Rachel eased closer to where Alex was restrained. Just being close to him helped to steady her frayed nerves. She turned slightly and he did the same. As she glanced at him, so many raw emotions surged through her. She'd spent so long trying to deny what she felt for Alex. The anger and bitterness in her heart didn't cover up the truth. Alex was important to her. Her entire past was mingled with his. How could she just write him out of her life simply because things hadn't worked out between them? She smiled up at him and for a second, it was just the two of them. And she was sure that she saw the same feelings she felt for him reflected on his face.

* * *

The look in her eyes warmed his heart. So many feelings had been left unsaid by them. He believed she still cared for him, no matter how ugly he had let things end between them. Was there still a chance? He was going to do everything in his power to find out. He wasn't about to let these men take that chance away, or lay the blame for their crimes on Liam. He'd die first.

So far, McNamara had no idea Alex was CIA, and he planned to keep it that way. He glanced briefly at the bed covering Deacon. So far, Deacon hadn't made a sound. Alex wasn't sure if that was good news or bad.

Hurry, Jase.

He wondered where Peter—aka Blake Temple—and the woman called Michelle were. McNamara was acting as if he was the boss, yet Alex didn't believe Temple would allow that to go on for long. From what Jase had told him about Temple, he wasn't the type to let someone steal his glory.

"We ran into two of your people in the woods earlier. Peter and Michelle. They were easy to capture." Alex hoped to get some reaction out of McNamara.

Something slipped briefly on McNamara's face, assuring Alex he knew Peter and the woman.

"I don't know who you are talking about. We don't know anyone by those names. Maybe they're working for Carlson."

McNamara motioned to several of his men and they went outside, leaving two more to stand guard. What were they doing?

He noticed Rachel's attention kept going to the bed where Deacon was hiding. "We have to help him," she mouthed.

So far, the two men guarding them didn't appear interested in what they were doing. As Alex's thoughts churned in a dozen different directions, he struggled to recall how many men there were in total.

If he was remembering correctly, it had to be more than twelve all together, which meant they were grossly outnumbered. With their hands restrained in front of him, there was no way they could take them all on, yet they desperately needed to draw the men's attention away from the cabin and Deacon.

The door opened once more and McNamara and the other men returned. "Just go along with them for now," he mouthed to Rachel. They needed to see what McNamara had up his sleeve. He prayed they weren't making a huge mistake by not making one final stand.

McNamara didn't waste time. He strode up to

Rachel, his anger evident in each step. "Time's up. Where is he?"

She squared her shoulders and didn't answer, fueling McNamara's rage.

"If you don't want to go to prison yourself, I suggest you start talking. Where is your brother?" he demanded, his face flushed with anger.

As a trained agent, Rachel knew not to react to his anger. "I don't know where Liam is. He didn't tell me where he was going."

McNamara clearly didn't believe her. "Don't give me that. You're lying. I know Carlson visited you. He told you something. What was it?"

Alex could see Rachel struggling to come up with a believable answer. He had to help her. "I'm Liam's friend. He never mentioned anything to me about where he was going, either. What you're accusing him of is preposterous. Liam would never betray his country."

McNamara gave him the once-over. For a moment, it was almost as if he recognized Alex, yet Alex was positive they'd never met before.

Still, McNamara's interest was now on him. "Then why are you here, if your friend did nothing wrong?"

"I'm here to help Rachel look for her brother," he told the man. "She hasn't spoken to Liam in over a week. She was worried."

McNamara's gaze narrowed as he continued to stare at Alex. "You're from here then?"

Alex hesitated before answering. "Yes, originally."

"Then perhaps I should be asking you where your friend is hiding. It would be better for him if he comes in peacefully. If we have to hunt him down it could turn...deadly."

The threat was clear. Before Alex could answer, a noise from where Deacon was hidden took McNamara's attention from him.

He stared at the bed. "What was that noise?"

Alex had to think fast. He couldn't let them examine the bed. "Wait, I think I may know where he is." He turned to Rachel. "You remember that one place where we used to hunt up here as kids?"

He watched her struggle to grasp the meaning of what he was trying to tell her. They'd hunted deer since they were kids, but only a couple of times up this way. Alex remembered the one time when they'd tracked some deer up to a particular spot.

It wasn't much to run with, but if they could talk McNamara and his men into going there, they'd get them away from Deacon. Possibly find a way to overpower the men left behind.

"Oh, right," Rachel said, as if it had finally dawned on her. "Liam loved that place. It would be the perfect place to hide, too. I can't believe I didn't think of it."

McNamara's interest riveted back to them. He'd forgotten all about the noise.

The man looked first at Rachel and then Alex as if smelling a trap. "You'd better not be trying anything or I'm telling you both, you won't like the outcome." The warning played uneasily through Alex's thoughts.

"We're not trying anything." Rachel pulled off the story completely. "But you have to promise you won't hurt my brother."

McNamara snorted. "I can't make that promise. Your brother will get what he deserves."

"Then I'm not telling you the location." She looked him straight in the eye.

McNamara stepped closer, once more trying to intimidate. "You are in no position to make demands as I see it."

Rachel didn't waver and eventually McNamara gave in. "All right, we'll do our best to keep him safe. Now, tell me where he is." Unfortunately, it was a hollow promise, given by a thug. Alex had little doubt that they'd kill them all once they had what they wanted.

"There's an old lodge up here that used to be popular when we were kids. It's been vacant for years now. It's warm and there are plenty of places to hide out. I think he would go there."

McNamara still wasn't convinced she was telling the truth. "Then you'll show us where it is." He yanked her toward the door.

Without thinking, Alex went after him. "She told you what you wanted to know. Let her go."

McNamara shoved him away. "You think I'm that naive? You two are planning to escape the minute we're gone. She's coming with me. That way I know you'll be here when I get back. You'd better not be lying," he barked at Rachel.

The man started for the door once more. Alex wasn't about to let him leave with Rachel. He didn't trust McNamara not to kill her. "Then I'm coming with you."

McNamara turned, looking at Alex as if he'd lost his mind. "If you're taking Rachel, you're taking me, too." Alex stood his ground. There was no way he was leaving Rachel at the mercy of these thugs.

NINE

"No, Alex." Rachel's gaze locked on Alex. She was terrified McNamara would shoot him right where he stood.

McNamara continued to glower at Alex while Rachel's heartbeat hammered against her chest. *Please don't kill him...* A disjointed prayer sped through her mind. She wasn't even sure what she was praying, only that she was certain God knew their needs and would protect them.

"Fine, you'll come with us," McNamara said in a deadly low tone. "But you'd best remember that you're expendable. I wouldn't suggest you try anything funny." Rachel's gaze clung to Alex. She would give anything to be able to understand the unspoken emotions simmering in his eyes right now. Would there ever be a right time for them?

Please, God.

McNamara nodded to one of his men, who

grabbed Alex by the arm. They were both forced outside.

When the final man left the cabin, Rachel found comfort in the fact that McNamara and his thugs hadn't discovered Deacon. At least he was safe for the moment.

Outside, the predawn had finally arrived and bits of filtered light pierced through the trees.

Two black SUVs slowly made their way to the camp. One of the drivers got out and hurried over to McNamara.

"We haven't found either of them yet." Rachel just managed to catch the man's words. Were they still looking for Liam and Deacon? If so, then at least there was hope that Liam was still alive.

McNamara was clearly irritated by the news. "Have your men keep looking. They can't have disappeared into thin air. Find them."

The man appeared scared of McNamara. He nodded and hurried back to the SUV.

McNamara turned his annoyance to Rachel. "Your brother has caused us enough trouble. You'd better know where he's hiding, otherwise it won't be good for you." Whatever it was that Liam had taken, McNamara was consumed with getting it back.

He opened the back door of the remaining SUV, flipped the seat down, and shoved her inside to the third-row seating. Seconds later, Alex was thrust in next to her. There was barely room for both of them to sit. Two men climbed into the back seat, keeping a careful eye on them.

With McNamara in the passenger seat, he pinned his gaze on Rachel once more. "Now, tell us where this lodge is and don't try to pull anything."

Rachel inched closer to Alex. She wasn't alone. No matter what happened, what they faced from here on out, she wasn't alone. "It's down the road we were on, halfway back to the town of Hendersonville. This road hasn't been maintained in years, though. We may not be able to make it the entire way by vehicle."

McNamara didn't answer. He motioned to the driver, who put the SUV in gear and slowly eased it down the slippery road.

Alex touched her hand and she looked at him. "We have to create a distraction to get away," he mouthed. She understood. Once they reached the lodge and discovered Liam wasn't there, McNamara would know it was a ruse.

Rachel struggled to recall the layout of the land, looking for something that would give them an edge over their captors. This side of the mountain usually got a lot more snow and ice accumulation. The patches she and Alex had run into earlier while fleeing would make traveling difficult.

Still, they needed help. God's help. She desperately prayed for divine intervention.

The driver didn't appear familiar with driving in the icy mountain terrain. His nervous reaction each time he hit a slippery spot on the road made it clear he wasn't comfortable with the conditions.

As he rounded one of the tight curves in the road, the vehicle began to slide. The man quickly overcorrected, heading them straight toward a sheer drop-off. He struggled to regain control of the ride while McNamara was screaming at him. The driver finally managed to rein in the vehicle, but not before blowing a tire after he drove the SUV over several jagged tree stumps.

When the vehicle finally came to a jarring stop, McNamara commenced verbally berating the driver for his failings.

"Well, what are you waiting for? Someone get that tire changed. Time is running out. We need to find him and get the…stuff." McNamara caught himself before giving more away.

The two men in the back seat hopped out along with McNamara and the driver, momentarily leaving Alex and Rachel alone.

Alex turned to her. "This is our chance. We

have to get out of here now. It won't be easy with these." He held up his hands.

Rachel glanced behind them, where one of the men had unloaded the spare tire and jack from underneath the SUV.

"I think they left keys in the ignition. If I can get up there without them seeing me, I'll try to drive us out of here. It'll be slow going, but they're on foot. We have a chance."

It was a long shot, but one they had to take. "I'll keep watch for you."

Alex slowly eased to the front seat undetected. He got into the driver's seat. "The keys are here. Hold on, this is going to be a rough ride."

Alex locked the doors, grabbed the keys, which proved difficult enough with his hands tied together, and then fired the ignition. He shoved the vehicle into Drive.

"They're getting away. Stop them!" McNamara yelled.

Rachel watched as all four men charged after them. "Hurry, Alex. They're coming."

Alex floored the gas pedal. The SUV lurched forward, the blown tire and his restraints making the ride ten times worse.

"Can you make it up to the front seat? We need to find a way to get these ropes off."

"I'll try." Rachel struggled to ease over the

seat with her hands tied. She landed halfway between the seat and floor and righted herself. After fumbling with the glove box, it finally opened. "There's a knife, a flashlight and a lighter inside."

Alex somehow managed to keep the vehicle moving forward in spite of the tire.

Rachel peeked behind them. The men were still coming after them. With the SUV's slower speed, they'd never get away from them like this.

She couldn't get the knife into a position to loosen her ropes. "Let me try to get yours free." With the blown tire and the rough road, the knife almost flew from her hand several times. Finally, she was able to cut through the rope and free his hands.

Alex rounded another curve and the road stretched out in front of them. Even with the bum tire, they were able to put distance between themselves and the men.

"I'm not sure how much farther we can make it in this thing. The engine's overheating because of the stress of pushing it so hard." He glanced behind them. "At least we appear to have lost them for now." As if in answer to his words, the engine sputtered and coughed several times before dying.

Alex took the knife from her and cut her free.

"Let's get out of here while we still can," Rachel said.

Alex shoved the knife and lighter into his pocket and grabbed the flashlight. Once he was by her side, they raced into the woods for their lives.

Alex grabbed her hand and they took cover in the nearby trees. "If we can stay out of sight, we might stand a chance."

"What should we do about Deacon?" Rachel asked. "He really needs help, Alex."

The men had taken their weapons and phones. They had no way to contact Jase or anyone else to get aid to Deacon. "We can't go back and risk leading them to him again. Let's just hope Jase was able to get airborne and will reach us soon."

Rachel grabbed his arm. He glanced at her and she pointed to the right. "I hear them," she whispered.

Alex froze where he stood. His arm circled her waist, tugging her close. He could hear McNamara yelling at his men.

"They can't be far. The SUV's right there. Search the woods. Find them!"

"Alex, we can't get captured again. They'll kill us."

"Let's get out of here," he said, and they headed deeper into the woods at a fast pace, while behind them, Alex heard the men enter the treed area.

Rachel stopped suddenly and he turned back to her. "Do you remember the summer we discovered that one cave up here?" she asked. It took him a minute to recall what she was talking about.

"I do. It's not far from here, if I remember correctly."

She nodded. "It is. If we can make it there, we can get out of sight. We'll disguise the entrance so that they won't know where we've gone."

It was a good plan and it just might work. When they'd discovered the cave, they'd spent the day combing through its tunnels and had never reached the end. It would make the perfect hideout. Would they find Liam there?

They were almost right against the mountainside now. Alex gathered his bearings. For the life of him, he couldn't figure out the direction of the cave.

"Which way?" he asked, hoping she knew.

She looked around. "Over there." She pointed to the right and then glanced behind. He could hear the men coming. They'd be right on top of them soon.

"They're almost here." He took her hand and they ran the rest of the way.

Finding the entrance after so many years

wasn't easy. It took a few minutes but he finally located it.

"Here, take the flashlight and go inside. I'll do my best to cover the entrance before they get here."

She took the light from him. "You won't have much time. Hurry, Alex."

Rachel went inside and he gathered armfuls of nearby brush and brought it over. He stepped inside the cave and piled the brush in behind him.

Please let it be good enough.

Rachel flashed the light down one of the corridors. "Let's get as far away from the entrance as we can just in case they spot the opening and check inside."

They headed down the corridor together. "Do you remember where this one goes?" he asked, and watched her smile at the memory.

"I do. There's that underground pool a little ways from here. Remember, we spent that same summer coming up here to swim. Liam never did figure out where we disappeared to."

He remembered that summer as clear as if it were yesterday. It was when he and Rachel had first started dating and they'd wanted to spend time alone. Liam had grumbled, feeling neglected by his best friend and sister.

"I remember Liam was so mad at us," he said,

and chuckled quietly. As he recalled, there was no way out beyond the pool and he told her this. "We need to go another way. It wouldn't do to get trapped in here."

They backtracked slightly and headed down another path.

"I was close enough to hear the exchange between McNamara and one of his men. He said they hadn't found it yet. They're looking for something other than Liam."

It certainly made sense. "I'm guessing this has something to do with what Liam took from them. That's why they need to find him."

"That'd be my guess, too." She shook her head.

They'd been walking for a while when Rachel stopped and listened. "Did you hear that?"

He did. It sounded like wind rustling close by. "Maybe there's another way out that we never found." They hurried toward the noise.

"I sure hope so. We need something to break our way."

Alex stopped in front of a small opening in the side of the mountain, barely large enough for them to squeeze through.

"We should be okay." Rachel looked up at him. "From what I can tell, we should be on the south side of the mountain. Some distance from where we last saw them."

He sure hoped so. Alex eased through the opening and looked around. Nothing stirred beyond the wind. "It's safe."

Rachel followed him out. "Looks like we've lost them for now, but they could have other men searching the woods. Alex, this thing is way over our heads."

He understood her frustration. He wasn't sure what the men were after, but he had a feeling it was deadly.

"We need to get to a phone and try to reach my team. Let them know the woods are crawling with men. They could be flying straight into an ambush."

TEN

Rachel's unsettled thoughts were torn between making sense of what they'd been through so far and untangling her feelings for Alex.

"Rachel?" She realized Alex had been trying to get her attention for a while.

"I beg your pardon?"

Something unreadable crossed his face. It made her wonder what he was thinking. "I said what if Liam actually *is* hiding at the lodge? We could be leading them straight to him. We need to reach the lodge before they do."

She hadn't considered it when she'd told them about the lodge, but it was possible. Liam loved the old place and there were many times when he went there to seek solitude. "I sure hope not. It depends on whether or not he's injured."

"I'm pretty sure Liam was the one who took care of Deacon. He'd try to get help. If McNamara and his men took Liam's phone and obviously Deacon didn't have one on him, then the only option for Liam would be to hike out…unless he couldn't."

They were racing against the clock, unarmed and running for their lives. If they didn't get help soon, those men back there would quickly catch up with them.

Rachel struggled not to let the helpless feelings overwhelm her. She'd been in countless situations just as deadly before, but she wasn't part of that life anymore and going back to it was difficult. She had to stay focused on saving Liam's life because the thought of losing her brother to these thugs was unimaginable.

"Hey." Alex stopped walking and took her hand, tugging her closer. He'd clearly seen all her fears. "Help is on the way and there's no way on earth we're giving up on Liam."

She forced a smile. "I know. I just feel so frustrated." She looked up at him. The expression in his eyes made breathing painful.

Alex gently framed her face. "Rachel," he whispered so softly and then leaned his head against hers. "I've wanted to tell you something for a long time now…" He hesitated, unsure. "I'm sorry for the way things ended between us."

She flinched as if he'd struck her. His regret was the last thing she wanted. She tried to pull away but he didn't let her.

"No, listen." The urgency in his voice made her want to hear what he had to say. "I should never have let you go," he whispered with so much passion that she believed him.

But did it matter anymore?

"I was messed up back then. I thought my life revolved around the CIA and you wanted me to walk away from all of that." He shook his head. "I was wrong. So wrong, and I've regretted the decision every day since."

Five years ago, she would have been thrilled to hear him say that. Now, it was just another reminder of what was lost.

Rachel moved away. Slowly, he let her go. "It's okay. Things happen for a reason. Maybe we wouldn't have worked out. I wouldn't have met Brian and I couldn't imagine my life without him. I think our lives turned out the way God wanted them to."

She watched him try to cover up the hurt. "I guess you're right," he murmured, and then turned away. When the awkward silence between them became too much, Rachel started walking again. Best not to reopen those old wounds again. Especially when their lives and Liam's were still in danger.

In the past, she'd tried to hold on to the fond memories of her life with Brian and shove aside the heartache of losing Alex. Although her husband had never questioned her about the relationship with Alex, she'd told him everything.

"How did you two meet, anyway?" Alex asked after a while, probably to fill the uncomfortable silence between them.

Rachel didn't really want to talk about her husband with Alex, but he had asked. "At church," she told him. "Brian attended the same church as Tom and Jenny. After I'd been home for a while, the Reagans invited me to go to the service with them." She stopped, remembering that dark time in her life.

She'd felt so lost. Couldn't believe it was possible to move forward with her life after losing Alex. Brian had taught her that no matter what circumstances you were going through, you could overcome them with God's help.

Brian's exuberant personality always made her smile. "He had leukemia when we met and yet you would never have known it from the way he presented himself. He was always smiling and happy. He was dying and he knew it but he never let it bring him down. He was an amazing man and I miss him terribly."

Rachel hadn't realized how much she'd loved Brian until he was gone. If his death had taught her anything, it was that it was possible to move on with your life no matter what you faced. She knew Brian wouldn't want her to be sad forever.

In fact, that had been his dying wish—that she not mourn for him too long. He wanted her to get on with her life. Be happy. She'd been trying to fulfill that promise to him ever since his death.

Seeing Alex again had brought all the old hurt to the surface once more. Was it possible for them to be able to move beyond the pain and regain the friendship they once shared? Could she accept being friends with Alex after everything they'd once had? She still cared for him, there was no doubt about it. Theirs had been a passionate romance. Could she settle for anything less?

Alex swallowed back the ache he felt when he looked at the love in Rachel's eyes for another man.

He could see she was still hurting. It was evident whenever the conversation returned to their past. Would there ever come a time when they could talk about what happened? He sure hoped so.

"We should be getting close to the lodge," she told him, and he roused himself.

He managed a nod. "Good. Let's hope Liam is there and that he's not injured too badly. We'll need to get him out as quickly as possible before McNamara and his men show up, which is only a matter of time."

"I can't even imagine what they're planning." Rachel shook her head. "And where are Temple and Michelle?"

He didn't want to say it aloud, but he believed whatever Temple had planned, it would involve deadly sarin gas.

"Right now, nothing makes sense and I'm too tired to try to fit the pieces together," Rachel said. "I'll leave that up to your team."

Under the best of conditions, the hike up Midnight Mountain was a physically challenging test. Having to run for their lives tripled the strain of the journey.

Alex stopped when he spotted the full round-log lodge in the clearing up ahead. "There it is." It had been years since he'd last been up here. Even back then, the place had been showing signs of decay.

They hurried past the overgrown parking area and stepped up on the porch. It had more boards missing than were still intact. Alex peered through one of the grimy windows. Years of dust and cobwebs blanketed the floor and the remaining furniture inside. He tried the door. Locked. The windows, as well. Were they wrong about Liam being here?

The temperature outside had dropped considerably with the growing cloud coverage, and the threat of snow loomed. It had to be well below freezing.

He and Rachel trudged through piled-up snow on the north side of the lodge around to the back and tried the doors and windows. All locked, yet someone had broken one of the windows.

Please let it be Liam.

Alex carefully removed the remaining slivers of glass and crawled through the broken window. It was only slightly warmer inside but at least it offered protection from the wind and snow. Several hours had passed without any sign of the men who'd taken them hostage, and yet he didn't doubt for a minute that they were still coming.

Alex unlocked the door and opened it for Rachel. "We need to search the place quickly. We won't have much time before they get here."

She glanced around. "There are so many rooms. We'll need to split up."

Rachel was right. They'd never get through the place otherwise.

"I'll take the upstairs. You search down here." She started to leave, but he reached for her hand, holding her there. All of her uncertainties were reflected on her face. "Be careful. I don't want anything to happen to you, too."

She swallowed visibly and then slowly smiled. "I will. You be careful, too."

While she began the downstairs search, Alex took the crumbling stairs two at a time. He and Rachel and Liam had been here many times in the past, so he knew there were only guest rooms up here. The time sitting vacant had taken its toll on the place, even more since the last time he'd visited it. Everything was showing signs of deterioration, and there were patches in the ceiling where Alex could see the sky. The weather and the elements were slowly reclaiming the place. A few more years and there wouldn't be much left.

After a thorough search of the rooms, there was no sign that anyone had been up there in a while. Was he wrong about the broken glass? It might have been broken years ago. Maybe Liam never made it this far?

Alex hurried back downstairs to help Rachel finish the search. He'd reached the kitchen area when he heard it. A footstep!

He found Rachel. Before she could say a word, he held his finger up to his mouth then pointed outside. She understood and frantically looked around for someplace they could hide. An enormous stone bar covered the length of the room, dividing it from the great room. She indicated the bar and they ducked below it.

Someone stepped up on the front porch. Liam? Another set of footsteps proved him wrong.

"I'm not so sure they'd come here," McNamara growled. "I think they were bluffing, trying to throw us off."

After a moment of silence, the second man said, "Looks like someone's been in there. They broke out the window."

McNamara said something unintelligible, then, "Hang on. The boss wants us to stand guard. The rest of the team is on their way. They have something."

If he and Rachel wanted to stay alive, they had to find another way out before the other men arrived.

Alex pointed to the hallway and Rachel nodded. They crept as low to the floor as they could while heading down the long passage. He opened the first door he came to as quietly as possible. It was a small bathroom with only a slatted window above the sink. Not enough room to escape.

Rachel opened another door. It led to what appeared to have once been the laundry room. There had to be another way out beyond one of the remaining doors. There was no way he was letting these men take them again.

Alex tried the final door on their left. It opened up to a large bedroom suite with French doors leading out to a wraparound deck outside. If his bearings were correct, they should be at the south side of the lodge facing the woods. Opposite from the men on the porch.

They moved to the doors and looked out. Alex couldn't see anyone. He said a quick prayer for their safe passage and slowly unlocked the door. It creaked as he opened it and he froze for a second.

Alex listened to make sure McNamara and the second man hadn't heard the door. He could hear them talking quietly. A good sign. He hoped it stayed that way.

ELEVEN

Rachel eased out behind Alex and around to the side of the lodge. She peered around the corner. Not a sound could be heard beyond the sporadic conversation from McNamara and his goon.

"We'll have to go slow, otherwise they'll hear us," she whispered.

Rachel stepped off the porch and Alex did the same. The snow lay deep in the woods behind the lodge, making the going slow. There would be no way to cover their tracks should someone happen this way, but the white blanket helped muffle the sound of their footsteps.

They'd barely covered any distance when the noise of an engine broke the silence of their surroundings. They stopped long enough to catch their breath.

Rachel's lungs burned from the cold air. "That must be the rest of McNamara's people."

"This place will be crawling with men in a few minutes." He looked at her, seeing the exhaustion she couldn't hide. "We have to go faster. Are you up to it?"

She wasn't so sure she was, but the alternative was impossible. "Yes, I'm up to it."

"The minute they find out we're not inside, they'll fan out and search the entire mountainside. We have to keep ahead of them."

They started walking as fast as the deep snow allowed through the woods. It took her a few minutes to realize they were heading back in the same direction as the camp.

"Do you think it's safe to go back into the camp?" Would they be leading the men back to Deacon?

"Probably not. But it's not safe to stay out here like this, either."

From the tree coverage where she stood, Rachel could still see the lodge. An SUV was now parked in front. It looked like the same one that had left the camp earlier.

As they watched, a second similar vehicle pulled up. Two people got out. Rachel recognized them right away. It was Blake Temple and Michelle.

"Alex, look." She pointed to the two. They watched as McNamara came out to meet them. From McNamara's body language alone, it was easy to see Temple was the real person in charge. McNamara had lied about not knowing Temple.

She couldn't make out what they were saying but it was obvious Temple wasn't pleased with the turn of events, and everyone was feeling the effects of his anger.

Several men who had been inside the lodge came out. She turned to Alex. "We need to get out of here. They know we're not inside."

He pointed in the direction of the cave they'd recently left. "I hate to keep backtracking, but it seems the safest and they don't know about the cave yet. At least we'll be out of sight. It will give us the advantage." He pointed to their footprints in the snow. "But first, we'll have to try to find a way to lead them away from the spot. They'll see our tracks and follow otherwise." Alex scanned the surrounding countryside. "This way." He pointed to their left. "There doesn't appear to be as much snow there and we can circle back to the cave easily enough."

They'd been able to slip through the cave unnoticed before. She hoped the same could be said for the return route.

"How much longer before your team arrives?" Rachel prayed it wouldn't be too late for Deacon and for them.

The bleakness in his eyes did little to encourage. "Depending on when they were able to get in the air, I'd say we have at least another four hours to survive."

Four hours! A lifetime when facing down death.

Alex saw her reaction and tried to be encouraging. "It could be sooner. Let's just get to the cave and out of sight as quickly as possible."

He was right. They were both unarmed. They needed to stay hidden.

As they hurried through the thick woods, a noise grabbed Rachel's attention. It sounded like…footsteps close by.

Alex heard it, as well. "Hurry, Rachel." He took her hand and they started running as fast as they could.

"Wait. Over there. I see them," someone yelled nearby. More than one set of footsteps could be heard stomping through the woods after them.

She glanced behind them. "They're gaining. We'll never make it to the cave."

Gunfire split the air and a round of bullets flew past her head. Rachel ducked low along with Alex.

Alex still held her hand. She looked into his eyes. "On my count," he said in a steady voice, and she slowly nodded. Once he'd counted off three, together they raced through the woods at breakneck speed with the men coming after them full force firing along the way. Were they trying to kill them? McNamara had said no, but the men's behavior spoke differently. If they no longer needed them alive, then had they found whatever they were searching for? Where did that leave Liam?

Alex stopped short when their path was blocked by a fallen boulder. It was the size of a small car and had sloughed off the mountainside.

Rachel stopped next to him. She couldn't believe it. They were trapped. "What do we do now? They're almost here."

"We surrender." She couldn't believe she'd heard this warrior beside her correctly. They'd barely escaped with their lives the last time. "If we want to live long enough to find Liam, we have to find out what this is really about once and for all."

Alex had just gotten the words out when four men came to a halt in front of them, weapons aimed at their heads.

"That's far enough," McNamara snarled at them. "You two, get them." He nodded to the two men on his right. One of the men rushed over and yanked Rachel by the arm, pulling it behind her back.

Anger boiled deep inside of him. Rachel had

suffered enough at these men's hand. "Leave her alone." Before he could reach her, the second man grabbed his arm, restraining him. "We're coming with you, okay? There's no need to hurt her."

"Be quiet." McNamara fumed at him. "You are in no position to tell us what to do. You two have caused enough trouble already…along with Carlson. You'd better hope when we locate him that he's willing to talk. Otherwise, none of you are walking out of here alive."

Rachel's gaze flew to Alex. He'd heard it, too. They didn't know where Liam was and whatever he'd taken was still missing.

As he'd learned so many times in the past, when your back was against the wall, God worked wonders. Alex prayed for God's intervention with all his heart.

"Search them both," McNamara ordered. Right away, the knife Alex had in his pocket was discovered and taken along with the flashlight.

"Get moving," the man holding Alex's arm ordered. "You've wasted enough of our time thrashing through the woods like this."

Rachel stumbled to the ground. The man gripping her arm dragged her to her feet. "I'm okay," she whispered to Alex when she saw the fear in his eyes he couldn't hide. "I'm okay."

She managed a smile, but he could tell she was running out of strength and hope. He understood. He was, too. It seemed that everything they'd tried so far had failed. They had no idea where Liam was and Deacon was in danger. Still, he wasn't ready to die here, and he certainly wasn't going to let anything happen to Rachel. He'd fight to his last breath to save her.

"Get them back to the lodge. He's angry. We need to get this thing settled now. Before they arrive," McNamara blurted out, and Rachel slid Alex a look. Someone was coming here? He tried to digest the meaning but he couldn't.

With two men restraining them and two others pointing weapons at them, Alex didn't believe he and Rachel stood a chance at taking them out. They'd be forced back to the lodge.

After what felt like forever, it came into view. Blake Temple stood on the porch. Where was Michelle? She'd been his constant companion and now she was no longer with him.

Rachel saw Temple as wel, and her footsteps faltered.

"It's going to be okay. Remember, they need us." Alex hoped that was still true.

Temple spotted them and hurried down the stairs. The men holding them captive released them and shoved them forward.

"So, we meet again." Temple's menacing

smile told Alex the man was going to enjoy getting even. "Well, this time the tables are turned." He addressed Rachel directly. "You will answer our questions now. Otherwise, your friend here will die."

Standing close to her, Alex could sense all her fears. She'd been through so much. He'd hurt her badly. She'd lost her husband too soon. She deserved to have the chance to be happy again, and he was determined to give it to her even if it meant losing his life to save hers.

"Where is he?" Temple got into her face. She couldn't keep from flinching. "We've searched the lodge. He's not here. Start talking."

While Rachel struggled to come up with a believable answer, he had an idea that just might work. "I know where he is," Alex told the man, immediately drawing Temple's glaring attention to him.

"What do you know? Who are you, anyway?" The man was clearly doubtful.

So far, no one appeared to know that Alex was CIA. He just needed to come up with a convincing story to buy them more time.

"Liam is my friend. He called me a few days before he went missing. I think I know where he would be hiding."

Faint interest showed on Temple's expression, yet he wasn't fully convinced.

"A friend, you say. What else did he tell you?" He was trying to figure out how much of the real story Alex knew.

"Nothing. Only that he was coming up here for a few days to fish in one of our old spots." The swimming hole in the cave. If he could convince them that Liam was in there, he and Rachel would have a shot at escaping through the labyrinth of passages the cave provided. The man who searched him earlier had taken the knife and flashlight, but had overlooked the lighter for whatever reason. They'd have the advantage. They knew how to get out. These men did not.

"Don't believe him. He lied to us before," McNamara told his boss.

While Temple didn't quite buy the story, whatever he needed from Liam had made him desperate. He was willing to go along. "And where exactly would that be?" Temple asked in a bristled tone. "And keep in mind, you'd better not be leading us on again…otherwise…" He left the threat hanging.

"I'm not. I want to live. I want Rachel to live. I know where Liam's at. I can take you there." Alex held on to a breath as the man continued to watch him, trying to determine if he was telling the truth.

"And why would you give up your friend?"

Alex struggled to make his answer seem believable. "Because I care about her and I don't want her to die because of something her brother did." He turned to Rachel, with his heart in his eyes. As he watched, a tear spilled down her cheek.

"Touching," Temple mocked. "Then you'll make sure you don't try anything foolish, because if you do, she dies." Temple turned to one of the men standing nearby. "Take him to the vehicle. I'll be there shortly." He faced Rachel again. "You'd better hope he's telling the truth. Otherwise, I'll kill you myself."

Temple motioned to one of his men, who grabbed Rachel's arm and started toward the lodge. There was no way Alex was letting Temple separate them. Staying together was their only chance at surviving.

"Hold on just a second. I'm not going anywhere without her." Alex stood his ground. He meant it. He wasn't budging without Rachel. "If you want my help, she comes, too."

Temple glared at him for the longest time. Alex was certain he'd call his bluff. "All right," he said at last. "But she stays in the vehicle, and if you're lying, I'll have my man kill her without thinking twice about it. Understood?"

Not exactly the answer Alex hoped for, but at least Rachel would be close. He struggled through exhaustion to come up with some way to get them both free. He couldn't help but feel time was running out. For them. Liam. Deacon. He couldn't imagine how bad Deacon's condition had deteriorated in the hours since they'd left him.

"Get them both in the SUV. We've wasted enough time. We have buyers counting on us."

Alex's blood ran cold. *Buyers counting on us*... Had Temple just let it slip that whatever it was they were trying to locate, possibly sarin gas, he had a buyer waiting impatiently for it?

He looked over at Rachel. She'd heard it, too.

"You men come with us. McNamara, try to reach them. Let them know everything is going according to plan," Temple told the man. "Apparently I can't trust any of you to do the job correctly. I'll need to go there in person to make sure Carlson gives up the location for the stuff."

Two men grabbed them by the arms and forced them into the back of one of the nearby vehicles.

Temple got up front along with a driver. The remaining two men sandwiched Rachel and Alex between them. They wanted to make sure they didn't try to escape.

Turning in his seat, Temple demanded answers. "Well? Where is this place? And keep in mind, I'm at the limit of my patience. If you can't produce your friend, you are no good to me."

The warning settled over him like a storm cloud. He knew what Temple meant. If they didn't come up with Liam soon, they'd be dead.

Alex told the driver where to find the entrance of the cave. "The vehicle won't be able to make it the entire way there. We'll have to go the rest on foot."

Temple clearly wasn't pleased by this, but he motioned the driver to begin. Once the SUV reached its limit, the driver stopped.

"Bring him with us," Blake ordered to the man closest to Alex. "You, keep an eye on her. If she tries anything, kill her."

"We'll get through this." Alex turned to look into her eyes. "Just like we did before." Realization dawned on her face. Praise God, she understood. If she could overpower her captor, she'd need to head to the second entrance. He'd try to meet her there.

He was forced out of the vehicle. There was just enough time for one final searching look between them before he was hauled away.

Temple stood in front of the vehicle, staring at the nearby mountain. "I don't see any cave," he muttered once Alex was forced to stop next to him. "This better not be another runaround like the lodge. This is your last opportunity."

"It's no runaround. The opening is hidden by grown-up scrub brush. It's this way, if I remember correctly," he added, so as not to tip the man off that he and Rachel had already been through the cave earlier and Liam wasn't there.

"Then what are you waiting for? Find it." Temple was furious. No doubt he had promised something that he was in danger of not being able to deliver.

After another quick glance back at Rachel, where he was almost positive he saw the tiniest of nods, Alex headed for the entrance to the cave with Temple and the other two men in tow.

He took longer than necessary to uncover the opening, while his limited options ran through his head. Once he'd shoved aside the brush they'd piled in front of the entrance, he noticed that their footprints were still there. He sure hoped Temple didn't spot them.

With the opening exposed, one of the men shoved Alex inside. He hit the opposite wall hard and winced in pain, holding his injured side.

"Well, which way to this fishing spot of yours?" Temple demanded as all three men entered the cave.

"To the left."

"Then lead the way," Temple ordered. "But

I'll warn you again, if you're lying, I'll kill you right here and she'll be dead soon after."

The chilling reminder of what was at stake shot through Alex's sleep-deprived mind. "It's dark this way. I'll need some light."

Temple stopped next to him. "You wouldn't be trying to warn your buddy now, would you?"

"I'm not trying to do anything but let you know there are some spots up ahead that can be hairy. If you're not watching what you're doing, you could break a leg."

After another glaring assessment, Temple motioned to one of his men, who used his phone's flashlight app to illuminate the cave.

The pool was still quite some distance from where they were. Alex headed that way while his brain started to formulate a clearer plan of attack. It was three against one. He needed something to level the playing field.

He remembered all the times he and Rachel had come up here in the past. The pool had been a surprise at first. He'd told Temple that Liam came here to fish, but that wasn't the case. The natural underground pool was cold as ice and there were no fish in it.

If he was recalling correctly, there was a small space just off to the right side that they'd only explored once a long time ago because it was unstable even back then. The walls were literally crumbling. If he could convince them to search in there...

When they reached the pool, the man with the flashlight app shone the light around the area. When it became evident that Liam wasn't there, Temple rounded on Alex. It was clear he was enraged. "You lied. There's no one here. And no sign that anyone has been here before. Enough. Kill him," he ordered one of the men standing close to grab Alex. The man reached for him.

It was now or never.

"I said he told me he was going fishing up here. We used to fish in this spot many times in the past. Maybe he gave up or... Wait, I think I hear something over there." He pointed to the small area.

Temple stared at the small dark space and then at him. "I don't hear anything."

Alex didn't look away. "I did. If he's injured, he could be hiding in there."

Temple motioned to the man with the flashlight. "Check it out."

The man didn't seem thrilled at the idea. Reluctantly, he did as his boss suggested.

Temple grabbed Alex's arm and hauled him along with him. The third man followed.

"Do you see anything?" Temple asked the man with the light. He let go of Alex and peered into the darkness.

Alex eased backward; the third man was now at his left side. His weapon was within reach. If he failed, he'd be dead…and so would Rachel.

In a split second, Alex grabbed the gun and shoved the man on top of Temple, sending them both sprawling into the room. Then he opened fire on the crumbling wall. It took only two shots before the ancient rock collapsed upon itself, entombing Temple and his men.

The world around him rumbled and shook. The place was unstable. He needed to get out of here as quickly as possible before the entire cave went down.

Alex stumbled in the direction of the entrance. The rumblings stopped. Dust boiled all around him. It wouldn't take long for Temple and his men to dig out. He had no doubt that the man guarding Rachel would have heard the noise by now.

He hurried out of the opening and spotted the man. He'd seen Alex. He jumped from the vehicle and began shooting.

Alex ducked behind a nearby tree. The man was coming his way. He returned fire, forcing the man to take cover behind the vehicle. One of Alex's rounds ricocheted off the front of the SUV. Right away, Alex could see fluid spilling out. The radiator was shot. The SUV was useless.

While the man continued gunning for him, in his peripheral vision, Alex saw Rachel ease from the vehicle. Before the man realized she was there, Rachel shoved him hard. He went sprawling across the frozen ground, his weapon landing in front of him. Rachel raced for the gun. The man grabbed her ankle and she fell. As she crawled and clawed for the gun, the man, still holding on to her ankle, reached it first. He snatched it with his free hand and pointed it at her head. She'd be dead in seconds.

Alex charged the man. When he spotted Alex, he turned the weapon on him. Before the man could get a single shot off, Alex fired once, striking the man through the heart. He fell backward, limp.

Now freed, Rachel grabbed the man's gun then felt for a pulse. "He's dead." She searched his pockets. "Alex, he doesn't have a phone." Frustration laced her voice.

"It doesn't matter. Let's get out of here while we still can. The SUV's useless and it won't be long before Temple and his men come after us." As they headed away from the site, Alex told her what had happened inside the cave. "We just have to stay out of sight for a few more hours. This is almost over."

He didn't say as much, but if the chopper ran into any obstacles along the way, it could be even longer before Jase and the team reached them. And he wasn't sure how much longer they could survive up here on the mountain on their own.

TWELVE

They couldn't keep running around without direction. Going back down the mountain wasn't an option with Temple's men still stationed at the lodge. She told Alex as much.

He seemed to be reading her thoughts. "We can't head back to the camp. That's one of the first places they'll look. I would if it were me. I just hope they don't find Deacon this time." He looked around the area, frustrated.

Rachel stopped dead in her tracks. "Wait, I can't believe I didn't think of it before now. The ranger station is up here on this side of the mountain."

He stared at her for a moment, not seeing the significance. "You mean the one on top of the mountain."

"Yes, but there's a radio up there. We can use it to reach the rangers and have them contact your people. Let them know where to look for us. We can get Deacon the help he needs." She didn't believe there was any way Temple's men would be looking for them up there. "They'll be expecting us to try to get off the mountain, not go farther up."

"You're right, they won't be. The only problem is it's at least a three-hour hike uphill and we're worn-out. My team may arrive before then…and I'm not sure Deacon has that long."

She shook her head, discouraged. "What other choice do we have? If they catch us again, they'll kill us, and it's too risky to try to get Deacon out of there on foot."

They'd be sacrificing Deacon's life by making the wrong decision.

Alex stopped next to her, apparently seeing all her concerns. He drew her close for a moment. "You're right. It's our only option. God didn't bring us this far to let us die. We have to hold on to that promise."

As she looked into his eyes, she believed him. Alex had dropped everything to help her find Liam and now, faced with death himself, his faith never wavered.

A breath separated them. As she lost herself in his eyes, something shifted inside of her. All the wishes she'd buried deep in her heart rose to the surface. She would always care for Alex no matter what happened in the future. She cupped his face. Everything she still felt for him was right there in her touch.

The years melted away, and it was like turning the clock back to the time when they'd dated. Her heart beat crazily against her chest. She'd give anything if this moment were happening under different circumstances.

She pulled away and stared up at him. She didn't want to hide her feelings any longer.

He gently stroked her cheek. "We should keep going. It's too dangerous to stop now…" Yet he didn't move.

Rachel swallowed visibly. Would there ever be a right time for them? The past seemed to determine that there wouldn't be.

She stepped away and he let her go. Regret was in his eyes.

"You're right. We have to keep moving." Rachel turned and stared up at the top of the mountain, where the ranger station was situated, trying to reclaim her composure. She'd loved him for as long as she could remember, but it seemed as if circumstances were determined to stand in the way of their having a life together.

As they continued hiking at an exhausting pace, Rachel struggled to think of where Liam might be hiding. Her gut told her he was still up here somewhere. Otherwise, the entire area would be crawling with agents by now. They'd covered many of the places Liam liked to go as a child, and yet her brother was still missing. She had little doubt that Liam was the one who had brought Deacon to the cabin and then he'd disappeared into thin air.

With no answers coming, she shifted her attention to what they'd overheard. "Temple said he wanted McNamara to let someone know that things were going according to schedule. He had to be talking about selling whatever Liam had taken from him. My guess would be sarin gas. Yet I don't understand how they managed to get it here in the US?"

They had to figure out who Temple's buyer was before it was too late. She was out of breath and running on her last ounces of energy. Thinking clearly was a near impossible task.

Alex looked about as worn-out as she was. Once they reached the ranger station, they could radio for help, but if Temple's men tracked them, there was nothing but a sheer drop-off behind the station. She didn't want to think about that possibility.

"What if they didn't bring the gas here?" Alex's voice interrupted her burdened thoughts. "What if they made it themselves?"

The possibility of Temple manufacturing the gas himself hadn't crossed her mind. She remembered Alex had told her that Temple and his men had been chasing the Chemist, the person responsible for manufacturing sarin gas.

"What if they found the Chemist and killed him? Decided to take over his business? They'd have his recipe for creating it," Alex said.

A shiver ran down her spine. "It's unimaginable that someone who is sworn to protect would do such a horrific thing."

"Yes, but there's no doubt in my mind that Temple and his goons are dirty. They've been doing who-knows-what unimaginable things since they faked their deaths. They're capable of this and a whole lot more."

She didn't doubt it for a second. "How do you think Liam got turned onto their crimes?"

Alex stopped for a breath. "Probably through his investigation of the new terror threat. That led him to these guys. I'm guessing Deacon may have been responsible for bringing them together."

It was beginning to add up. Liam had been searching for a link to tie the gas to his new threat. Deacon might have been working undercover with the Chemist or even with Temple.

"What about Michelle? Where does she factor into all of this?" Rachel asked as they started walking again. It was hard just putting one foot in front of the other.

Alex ran a hand across the back of his neck.

"Her I can't figure out. I felt as if she was frightened of Temple and yet when she had the chance, she didn't accept our help. In other words, I don't know." He barely managed a shrug.

Guilt tore at her. He'd put his life on the line and they were still no closer to understanding what was happening than when they'd started on his mission. She touched his arm and he stopped, looking at her curiously. "I'm so sorry I got you involved in this. I didn't know who else to trust. Liam's note scared me."

His handsome face twisted in pain. "No, Rachel, don't apologize. Liam is my family...and so are you." His green eyes softened as they swept over her face, the look in them reminding her of the man she'd once loved...the one she still loved.

You never forget your first love...

She swallowed back the hurt that realization brought. He stepped closer. She did, too. He was going to kiss her. She so wanted to feel his lips against hers again, but she was barely hanging on as it was. She wasn't ready to face the truth just yet. She stepped away. Saw his wounded reaction, but she couldn't go there. Not now. Not yet. She wasn't even sure they would survive the day, much less if she could survive Alex's leaving her again.

"I'm sorry," he whispered in a broken tone. "Are you okay?"

She couldn't look at him. "I'm fine. It's just… working with you again has brought up some old feelings I thought I'd dealt with."

He didn't say anything. The uncertainty in his eyes had her full attention. This was not Alex. He had never seemed so unsure before. "What is it?" she asked.

His gaze held hers. The pain she saw there was real. "Being with you again has made me realize what I lost when I lost you."

With her heart breaking, she bit down on her bottom lip to keep from crying. "We both made mistakes, but that's all in the past. We can't go back and fix it now, can we?" She loved him, but she couldn't open her heart up to that much hurt again. She'd lost too much in her life.

"I guess you're right." Regret hung in his voice. She understood. She had regrets, too. "We still have a long ways to go. At least we'll have decent cover at the ranger station. It'll get us out of the elements for a while."

Rachel couldn't answer for the longest time. It was a struggle to keep back the tears. It felt as if they were saying goodbye to each other all over again. "I guess you're right," she managed, and they both started walking again.

The farther they climbed up the mountain,

the more the snow piled up. Little sunlight got through the denseness of the wilderness up here.

Exhausted and barely hanging on, Rachel lost her footing on what appeared to be a downed tree. She started to slide back down the mountain but Alex caught her.

Without the proper hiking gear, they were at the mercy of the mountain. Yet one thing working in their favor was that the men chasing them didn't seem any better equipped for the hike than they were.

She looked behind her to see what she'd stumbled over and somehow managed to stifle the scream before it could escape. It wasn't a log. It was a man.

He'd been shot in the back of the head. There was a gaping hole there where his skull had once been.

Alex knelt and rolled the man over. Rachel recognized him. "That's Seth Jamison. Liam's handler. Alex, they killed Liam's handler. Which explains why I haven't been able to get in touch with him. What was he doing out here?" Her voice trailed off as the truth became apparent. Seth was the person on the inside helping Temple and his men.

"My guess is he was working for Temple. Something must have happened. Maybe Seth got a conscience and threatened to turn them in. They killed him because of it."

Rachel was in shock. "I can't believe it. Why would he do such a thing?" Something else occurred to her. "He betrayed Liam. Alex, he must have told Temple about Liam's meet. That's why they were ambushed. Seth almost got them both killed, and for what?"

Alex stared at the dead man. "I don't know. I can't believe someone Liam trusted was corrupt. But it explains a lot. Once Jase and the team arrive, we'll send someone down to retrieve the body. His family will need to be notified." Alex got to his feet and looked at her. "How are you holding up?" It was freezing cold and she was beginning to perspire. They couldn't afford to become hypothermic.

She shrugged, resigned. "I'll be okay. The sooner we get to the station, the better, though."

Alex didn't look convinced. "It's at least another hour if not more before we reach it. We need to find a place to warm up. Otherwise, we'll never make it."

Weary to the bone, she looked around, but there was no shelter from the elements. "We really need a fire."

Alex dug into his pocket and pulled out the lighter the men hadn't taken. "Let's see if we can find some sheltered trees to a build a fire so that we can warm our frozen limbs."

The sight of the lighter in his hand was like a prayer answered. "Oh, thank you. I can't feel my feet anymore."

He looked around, trying to find a safe place for the fire that would be obscured from sight. "Over there." He pointed to a group of trees. "It looks secluded enough. They shouldn't see it if they happen this way."

Alex dug out a spot in the snow to put the fire while Rachel gathered what loose branches she could find.

When the fire finally caught, they both moved in as close as they dared. Rachel could feel its warmth as she leaned in closer. Never had a simple fire felt so good. She closed her eyes with joy. "That feels wonderful."

Alex chuckled at her expression. "You're right it does. But we can't afford to stay here for very long. We have to keep one step ahead of them if we're going to make it out of this. And there's always the chance they'll see the fire and come check it out."

She understood, but she hated to leave the warmth. It was funny the things you took for granted. Like being warm enough.

"How much longer before your team members arrive, do you think?" she asked again, and couldn't quite keep the desperation from her tone.

"Not too much longer. The only problem is they have the coordinates for the camp. They won't know how to find us up here unless we can radio them from the tower."

He focused on the fire, no doubt weighing their impossible options. Rachel glanced his way. Alex was still the most attractive man she knew. He fit the part of a true hero right down to tall, dark and handsome. And she would always love him.

Alex caught her watching him, and her chest grew tight at the tenderness she saw in him. There was no denying the feelings still ran strong between them. But would it matter in the end if neither of them were able to walk off Midnight Mountain alive?

There was no doubt in his mind that he loved her. He'd never stopped loving her. She wasn't ready to hear those words from him. Would she ever forgive him, or had his actions all those years ago destroyed any hope they had for rekindling their love?

It was a hopeless feeling to be caught up in a situation so out of control and bordering on impossible like the one they faced right now. In his heart he believed that God had answered his prayer and was giving him a second chance to prove to Rachel how he felt about her. They just had to survive long enough for him to have that chance.

"How are you feeling?" he asked, trying to take his mind off their grim situation.

She turned to stare up at him, then slowly smiled. "Better, thanks. The fire really helped." Her smile still had the power to brighten his dark day.

"I'm glad. Are you ready to finish this?" She didn't hesitate before confirming with the smile still in place.

Together, they tamped out the fire then threw snow on top of it to cover the smoldering ashes. Once Alex was satisfied they'd hidden all evidence, they started up the mountain again.

Just having time to warm up and rest did wonders for his drained energy. He was ready to finish this thing once and for all, to find out the truth behind Liam's disappearance and hopefully convince Rachel to give him a second chance.

He still couldn't believe that Liam's handler had been working for Temple's crew. How long had Seth been betraying his country? Had he been involved with Temple's plan to fake his death? With Seth dead and Liam missing, the only chance they had for getting answers was through Temple.

Alex hadn't been able to get Liam's letter out of his head. There was no doubt in his mind that Liam was trying to tell him about the one specific location he'd underlined for a reason. He believed it was where Liam had stowed the sarin. He told Rachel his suspicions.

That realization dawned on her face. "It makes sense. I can't believe I never considered it before now. Alex, we can't let Temple and his men find those weapons. If they reach the cave before we do, then they won't need Liam or us."

Those frightening words hung uneasily between them. "Let's just hope they haven't found them already. They certainly have enough men out here to search the entire mountainside."

"Where is Liam?" Rachel shook her head, and Alex could see her frustration. "I can't help but believe he's up here somewhere still. There's so much territory to cover up here. It could take weeks to locate him. By then it will be too late."

He stopped walking and faced her. "You can't think like that. We need to trust God to take us to where Liam is." He did his best to sound convincing, but it was hard to keep positive after everything they'd been through. He wanted to believe God was directing their footsteps, but his faith was faltering.

Help my unbelief. The last thing he wanted was for Rachel to see him give up.

"You're right. I'm sorry. I'm just tired. Liam wouldn't give up on either of us if the tables were turned. I won't give up on him, either."

He tucked her hands in his. "Good. I can't help but think Liam had a backup plan in place when he came up here. Maybe he even had some supplies stashed somewhere. I know Liam. He's a stickler for details and he always was the most prepared of the three of us."

She smiled at the memory. "Yes, he was. He left me the map and his phone for a reason. The same way he left you that letter. Of course he'd be prepared for whatever came his way. He'd be expecting trouble. He *was* expecting it."

Her confidence in her brother was well deserved. Liam was a seasoned agent. He would be okay and so would they. Once they reached the ranger station, they'd radio Jase with their location. Praise God, this thing was just about over.

The thought had barely cleared his head when a noise nearby captured both their attentions and sent them running for the cover of a nearby grove of spruce trees.

Alex could make out voices. More than one and they were almost right on top of them.

"The boss said he saw smoke over this way. I don't see anything, do you?" There was no mistaking McNamara's voice.

Alex tugged Rachel closer. Her eyes were filled with an uncertainty that he couldn't begin to assuage. His own pulse was threatening to explode in his chest.

"Did you hear something?" one of the men asked in a somewhat uneasy tone.

"No, but you two check it out," McNamara ordered. "We can't afford to let them get away. Too much is at stake."

Alex heard footsteps coming toward their hiding spot. One of the men was almost directly in front of them. If he turned slightly, he would see them. If they were found now, his gut told him they wouldn't walk out of the wilderness alive.

He prayed with all his heart and left the fear in God's hands.

"There's nothing here," the man closest to them grumbled. "Come on, it's freezing up here. I don't see anything that resembles a fire, anyway. The boss must have been mistaken."

The second man stared straight at the tree they were standing behind, then abruptly turned on his heel. He and his partner headed back to where McNamara and another man waited.

"Let's get out of here. Chances are, they headed back down the mountain another way," McNamara told them. "We can still head them off before they reach the town and we have men waiting there if they give us the slip."

Alex clutched Rachel close as the noise of the men's footsteps slowly disappeared.

When he felt it was safe, he eased out from behind the tree with Rachel still tucked in his arms.

"That was too close," she whispered, her breath fogging the air between them.

"Yes, but it sounds as if they aren't expecting us to be here, which means they won't be looking for us up at the station. That's something," he managed without really feeling confident.

"It should give us time to finish the climb without looking back over our shoulder. Either way, let's keep pushing forward. We're almost there, Alex. We're almost there."

He brushed back some escaping hair from her face and looked into her eyes. There was still a lot of danger between them and getting the answers they wanted. He needed her to listen. He'd been holding these feelings inside for way too long and there was no promise of the future. They faced armed men, the elements of the mountain and physical exhaustion. There were no guarantees.

If they were caught, if they didn't walk out of this thing alive, he wanted her to know the truth. He loved her. He wanted to be with her. And he'd do whatever it took to convince her he was serious this time.

THIRTEEN

She held her breath, waiting for him to say something. Hoping he did. Praying he wouldn't. She couldn't lose her heart to him again.

His hands still rested on her shoulders. She couldn't take her eyes off him. "Rachel, I know things ended badly between us before because of me. I know I hurt you terribly, but I want you to know that I learned a lot after you left."

She tried to pull away, but he didn't let her. "No, wait."

She couldn't do this now and not fall apart. "Alex, please…"

"Rachel, look at me." Slowly, she did, because in spite of everything her heart desperately wanted to hear what he had to say. "I know I messed things up between us, but I'm not the same person I was back then. I've changed. *God* changed me," he amended, and she believed him. She'd seen this change in him.

"I'm not asking for you to forget what happened, and I don't expect you to answer me now, with our lives on the line like this. I just want you to know that I still care about you. I never really stopped caring."

Tears filled her eyes. She turned away and he let her go. Why now? Why did he have to tell her these things now, after all the heartache and pain she'd gone through? Why couldn't he have loved her the way she needed him to back then?

"Alex, I can't do this now." Her voice was little more than a broken whisper.

When he didn't respond, she looked at him. Her answer couldn't be the one he'd hoped for, yet he slowly agreed.

"Okay." Without another word, he started walking and, after a much-needed moment to regain her composure, Rachel followed, her thoughts disjointed. Her heart was in her throat.

Through the clearing in the trees, she could see the ranger station up ahead. They were almost there.

"Alex, look." She pointed up ahead and he followed her direction. The relief on his face was easy to read.

Just seeing the station gave them both an extra boost of energy. They were almost to the building when a debilitating thought occurred and she grabbed his arm.

"What if someone is waiting for us in there?" Rachel could tell he hadn't considered it.

They ducked behind a tree. "I can't see anything, can you?"

She squinted hard but could see nothing in the twilight of the wilderness. "There's no movement that I can tell. What do you want to do?" She was grateful that at least they were both armed now.

"Let's ease up to it. Try to stay in the cover of the trees as much as possible."

She nodded and waited until he'd made the first move and then she followed. Each step echoed in her ears. So far, there was nothing out of the ordinary. Still, they'd been through so much already. What if there were men waiting inside to finish the job?

Still some distance from the station, Alex stopped suddenly.

"Did you hear that?" He barely got the words out when the silence around them was shattered by an assault rifle discharging.

Rachel dove for the cover of the closest tree, with Alex in tow.

They hunkered low as the shots continued to ring out. With the distance between themselves and the person firing on them, it was impossible to make out anything about him.

"I only hear one shooter," she told him.

He listened for a moment. "You're right. Whoever it is, they're alone. Can you cover me? I'll try to circle around behind the station and go up that way. Maybe I can take him out."

She nodded, but before he left the protection of the tree, she stopped him. "Alex, wait."

He turned to her, those piercing eyes undoubtedly seeing what she could no longer hide. "I still care about you, too. I always have… I always will."

The joy on his face sent her heart soaring. Alex took her hand and slowly raised it to his lips. He held it for just a second longer and then slowly let it go.

She was more fearful than ever before. She had so much to lose. "Be careful," she urged, and he smiled down at her.

"I will."

She watched Alex run for the next tree up. The person firing on them was quick to spot his movements and another round of bullets kicked up the dirt near where Alex stood.

Keeping as flat as she could, Rachel edged around the tree and opened fire. She caught a glimpse of a man standing in the open station window before they ducked out of sight.

Alex took advantage of the down time and rushed to the back of the building. Once he was in place, Rachel would draw the shooter's attention away from him.

She aimed for the opening and fired off several rounds. She could see Alex slowly easing up the stairs. If she could keep the man's attention on her, Alex might be able to take him by surprise.

Rachel fired off several more rounds, giving Alex the time he needed to charge the station. She heard a brief scuffle, then silence. *Alex!* He needed her. She ran as fast as she could to give aid.

With her heart pounding out the rhythm of her footsteps, she took the steps two at a time.

Once she reached the landing, she was boosted by adrenaline every step of the way to the open door. The station consisted of one circular room that afforded a three-hundred-sixty-degree view around them.

Through the filtered light, she saw two men standing close. Something was wrong. There were no weapons drawn. Alex jerked toward her. As she drew near, the look on his face was one of sheer disbelief.

"What is it?" She barely managed to force the words out.

And then the second man slowly turned to her. Two things quickly became apparent. He was injured, his shirt covered in blood. She couldn't tell the extent of his wounds, but he'd obviously lost a lot of blood. The man staring back at her had Rachel dropping her weapon and running into his arms.

This was her brother. They'd finally found Liam and he was alive.

Alex watched as Rachel hugged Liam, and his exhausted mind struggled to take it all in. Liam was here. He was alive.

Liam staggered under Rachel's embrace and she pulled away, somehow managing to catch her six-foot, one-hundred-seventy-pound brother before he could fall.

"You're hurt." She slowly eased him to the floor. The amount of blood on his shirt was alarming.

Alex tucked his weapon behind his back and knelt next to Rachel as she carefully unbuttoned Liam's shirt.

"I'm okay. I bandaged it up, but we need to get out of here as soon as possible. They can't find it." Liam tried to get up but slumped back onto the floor.

Alex tried to quiet his friend. "We will. Help is on the way. I just need to let them know where to find us." He glanced around the circular room, looking for the radio. He spotted a flare gun and quickly pocketed it. But then he saw something that threatened to take away his last bit of hope. Someone had deliberately smashed the machine. His spirits sank.

"What happened to the radio?" he asked Liam.

Liam shook his head. "It was like that when I arrived. They must have beat me here. I guess they wanted to make sure I didn't have a way to call out for help." Liam winced in pain as Rachel did her best to secure the wound once more.

Alex had to know what Liam had found out. "Who are these people? Why are they after you?"

Liam seemed to be fighting to keep from losing consciousness. He'd lost a lot of blood and the exertion of trying to defend himself had taken its toll. "Former CIA," he murmured, before he closed his eyes. "They're all supposed to be dead."

The statement pretty much confirmed what he and Rachel had suspected.

Before he could ask another question, Rachel's worried gaze met his. "He needs immediate medical attention and I can't even imagine what's happened to Deacon by now."

Liam caught what she'd said. "Deacon? You've seen him? Is he okay?"

Alex couldn't lie to his friend. "He's in pretty

bad shape, but he's hanging on. You were the one who took him to the camp?"

Liam nodded weakly. "We were attacked. I'd been working with Deacon for a while. Through his asset, he found out where the sarin gas was stored and we managed to get it to a secure location. I was supposed to meet with Deacon's asset, who would give us the names of the people Temple and his men are selling sarin gas to, but we were attacked instead. We were taken hostage. They took our weapons and cell phones. I thought they would kill us, but they demanded to know where we'd moved the sarin. Deacon and I managed to escape, but not before we were both injured." Liam closed his eyes once more, breathing heavily.

Alex squeezed his friend's arm. "Rest now. I'm going to see if I can fix the busted radio."

He got to his feet and motioned to Rachel. She made sure Liam was as comfortable as possible and then she joined him.

"Do you think you can get it working again?" She glanced at the destroyed radio with doubt.

"I don't know. It's in pretty bad shape, but it may be our only way to reach Jase before it's too late."

"What do you need me to do?" she asked.

"Keep a watch outside. If they've been here before, and we have to assume they have because of this—" he pointed to the destroyed radio "—then there's a good chance they'll search here again. Especially after hearing the shots."

A noise behind them captured both their attentions. Something was wrong with Liam. His head slumped to one side. He was unconscious.

They rushed to his side. "Liam, buddy, wake up." Alex shook his friend gently. After an alarming amount of time had passed, Liam slowly opened his eyes. "Stay awake for me, Liam. I need you to do your best to stay awake."

Liam managed the smallest of nods. Rachel's reaction to seeing her brother's condition worsen was devastating. She was terrified of losing him.

Alex got to his feet and held his hand out to her. She couldn't take her eyes off her brother.

"Rachel, look at me." She stood as well, finally focusing on his face. "I need to see if I can fix the radio to get Liam help. I need you to stand guard…okay?"

Slowly, she agreed. She took up her weapon and went over to the opening that faced out to the grounds below. It showed the same path that they'd come up.

Alex went to work on the radio, using all his ham radio knowledge to try to bring the busted machine back to life.

While he worked, he couldn't help but feel that time was running out. With so many loose ends tangled around each other, they'd need a clear head and safer grounds to understand what was really going on here. He still couldn't believe former CIA agents who had once been honored for their work in the field were responsible for attacking Liam and Deacon along with himself and Rachel. They clearly had nothing to lose at this point.

He tried to sort through the details he knew so far. Temple and his thugs had sarin gas here in the US, which was unimaginable in itself. Whether or not they'd smuggled it in or produced the gas themselves was uncertain. Both he and Rachel had overheard Temple talking about a meeting with someone. A possible buyer for the weapons here in the US. Alex didn't like the sound of it.

Something Liam had said troubled him. He'd told them that Deacon was working with him and that they were supposed to meet with Deacon's asset, presumably someone connected to Temple. Did Liam's handler know about Deacon?

Alex knew very little about Jamison, other than what Liam had told him. According to his friend, Jamison was a stand-up guy and always had Liam's back. He trusted the man completely. Had Liam's trust been his downfall?

FOURTEEN

Trying to keep her focus on the grounds below was an almost impossible task. All she could think about was Liam. His condition was getting worse. She glanced back at her brother. Had they found him again only to lose him to his injuries before they could get him to safety?

Please, God, no.

She'd never seen Liam look so weak. He'd been shot before, but never like this. Liam had been her rock, especially after she'd lost Brian. Now Liam needed her and she felt so helpless.

Something caught her attention below. What looked like a light flashed. She quickly ducked behind the closest wall. She was almost positive it was the reflection of a gun scope.

Alex must have spotted her reaction because he hurried to her side, careful to stay out of sight of the opening. "Did you see something?" Concern creased his brow.

"There's someone out there. They're armed."

"Did you see how many?"

She'd only caught a glimpse. "I'm not sure. I just caught sight of the one person."

He looked back at Liam. "We need to try to keep him as quiet as possible. Maybe they won't look here again since they've destroyed the radio."

She so wanted to believe it. She didn't. These men were ruthless and they had everything to lose. They would have heard the shots from earlier. They'd know the direction they came from.

Rachel eased to the opposite side of the opening, careful to keep out of sight. Alex followed. She peered out. She could no longer see anything, including the rifle scope. Had she been wrong?

She watched as Alex searched the area below them then shook his head.

"I don't see the person anymore, either. I could have been wrong." She didn't believe it, though. There was someone out there. The only question remaining was how many of them there were.

He didn't answer. His focus was trained on something below. "Wait, I see something. There's at least three men coming this way."

She looked in the direction he indicated and spotted them. "We can hold our ground against them for a little while until we run out of ammo, but it's going to call a lot of attention to us. The rest of Temple's men will be here before your team has a chance to find us. There will be no escaping then."

Alex hurried across the room and looked down below. "Nothing but a sheer drop-off back here. There's a small ledge, which barely has room to stand and no room for error."

She understood what that meant. They'd have to try to hold off Temple's team until the Scorpions arrived.

Rachel grabbed Liam's weapon and checked the clip. He was almost out of rounds. Hers wasn't much better. It was only a matter of time before they were overthrown.

If they were going to die here, she wasn't letting that happen without telling Alex how she felt about him.

Alex headed for the opening where he'd seen the men, but she stopped him. "Alex, wait."

He turned back to her, searching her face.

Rachel slowly found the courage she needed. "Alex, we may not make it out of here and I can't die without telling you…how I feel about you."

She'd never seen him look so uncertain. He reached for her and tugged her close. His arms were everything that she remembered, but she needed to tell him everything.

"No, I need to say this."

He waited for her to go on.

"When you chose the job over me, well, it was crippling. I thought we would have a future together and then it just ended." She shrugged. She couldn't lose control now. "When I got back home, I was a wreck. I couldn't function for the longest time, but slowly, with Liam's help and the Reagans, I moved on. I married Brian because I cared about him. He knew all about you and me, but it didn't matter to him." She stopped for a breath. "I'll always be grateful for him, but I never stopped loving you, Alex. And I never will."

He framed her face with his hands and kissed her tenderly. When he looked at her the way he was right now, she was so afraid. She had so much to look forward to in life, and it might quite possibly be taken from her again.

"I'm not going to let that happen, Rachel," he said, reading her worried thoughts. "We will make it out of here, and when we do, we will have a lot to talk about. Do not give up on us." The sincerity in his eyes made her want to keep fighting with all her might.

She managed a smile for him. "I won't. I'll never give up on you again." With one final kiss, they both eased to the opening once more. The men had stopped. They appeared to be assessing the station carefully. She could see them talking, then one of the men slipped closer to the station.

"He's coming inside. If we can take him out, it might force the others to search for him. It will give us some leverage."

Rachel understood. She would act as bait for the man to draw his attention away from Alex, who would take the man down. She heard the first step below creak, followed by another. She'd been in situations like this hundreds of times in the past, yet the adrenaline rush of the life-and-death situation was always there.

A shadow fell across the door to the building. Rachel kept her hand on her gun. This was it. Their lives—their future—came down to her not losing her cool. The door slowly opened. She saw the barrel of the gun first. She waited for the man to enter. Her thoughts screamed that she didn't want to die here along with Liam and Alex without knowing what their sacrifice was all about.

Alex waited behind the door as the man eased through it. He barely cleared it when he spotted Rachel. Before he had the chance to fire off a single round to warn his comrades, Alex grabbed the man from behind in a choke hold. The man struggled like a wild animal. Alex tightened his hold around the man's neck. After what felt like forever, his struggles grew weaker. The weapon slipped from his hand. Rachel rushed to grab it before it could hit the floor. Once the man was unconscious, Alex eased him down to the floor.

"That didn't go as quietly as I'd hoped." He went to the opening and glanced down at the two men. They were definitely on alert.

Rachel joined him. "I'm not sure they heard him, but it won't be long before they come looking. At least for now, it's two against two."

It was something, he guessed, but how long before the rest of Temple's goons came after them?

Alex went back to the man and checked his pocket. He had a cell phone. "Thank You, God," he said in a grateful tone, before he punched in Jase's number. "Jase, it's me, Alex. I don't have much time." Alex knew his commander wouldn't recognize the number. As quickly as he could, he told Jase what was happening.

"We're still an hour out at best," Jase told him. "We ran into some sketchy weather. We'll head for the ranger station. In the meantime, I'm calling in the state troopers. I know you don't trust the local authorities, but these guys are state. Hang in there. This is almost over."

Alex ended the call with Jase's assurances running through his head.

He turned to Rachel and smiled. "They're close. He's calling in backup, too."

She went into his arms and held him tight. "I'm so grateful. I'm not sure how much more of this we can take on our own."

He kissed her temple and let her go. "I'll keep an eye on the guys below. You watch this one in case he wakes up."

Alex went over to the opening. One of the men had disappeared. He searched the area below. Where had he gone?

"What's wrong?" Rachel had noticed him looking around.

"One of them is missing. He may be heading this way."

She moved closer to the door. With the butt of the weapon ready, she waited, but nothing happened. After what felt like an eternity, she glanced over at Alex.

He shook his head. The man still hadn't appeared again. His buddy was standing behind a tree, partially visible. "I don't see him. Maybe he got worried about his missing comrade and went for help." If he had, then Alex wasn't sure they could hold the men off until Jase arrived.

"We can't afford to make a run for it with Liam's condition so serious."

Liam opened his eyes as if he'd heard her say his name. When he spotted the man lying by the door he tried to stand, but Rachel hurried over, trying to quiet him. "Liam, it's okay. Try to stay as still as possible. Help is almost here."

"That's one of the men who took Deacon and me hostage," Liam managed in a whisper. He glanced up at Alex. "There are others out there still, aren't there?"

Alex had to tell him the truth. "There are. Two more that we know of. I see the one, but the second is missing. He could be anywhere. Can you keep an eye on this guy?"

Liam didn't hesitate. "I can."

Alex smiled in spite of the situation. It had been years since he and Liam had worked together. He'd missed his companion.

Rachel clearly wasn't sure. "He's too weak, Alex," she whispered so that only he could hear. "He won't be able to withstand a firefight. Is there still no visual of the other one?"

Alex shook his head. He didn't like it. "They're definitely up to something."

He had barely gotten the words out when the second man appeared again next to his friend. "Where was he?"

"Something's wrong." Rachel looked through the scope of the weapon of the man she'd disarmed. "He has something in his hand."

Before she finished talking, the man's companion opened fire and they were forced away from the opening.

After the first round of shots whizzed past them, Alex aimed at the man who'd fired on them, forcing him back behind the coverage of the tree.

"Where's his friend again?" Rachel asked. Alex glanced below. The man had vanished again.

Uneasiness coiled into the pit of Alex's stomach. The shooter opened up on them again, forcing their attention from the opening.

Alex and Rachel returned his shots, but they were using up valuable ammo they didn't have to use.

"Hold your fire," Alex told Rachel. "They could be trying to run us out of ammo then charge the station."

She did as he suggested but kept a careful eye on the man behind the tree. "He's just standing there. Almost as if he's waiting on something."

"Or someone..." Alex's gaze latched with hers. She shivered visibly.

With the silent standoff continuing, Alex kept listening for any sound of the missing man approaching. What was he up to?

The thought had barely cleared his head when something came hurling through the opening.

Alex ducked to keep it from hitting him; the smell of gasoline was pungent.

Seconds later, the station exploded in fire. The man had thrown a Molotov cocktail into the building. The station went up like a tinderbox, filling the room with acrid smoke. Alex hurried to Liam's side and helped him to his feet. Their once-unconscious assailant was beginning to come to.

Alex pointed his weapon at him. "If you try anything, I'll shoot you. Do you understand?"

Coughing from smoke inhalation, the man glared at him.

"There's only three of them! You can take them!" the man yelled, trying to warn his buddies.

Alex took a step closer and he quickly shut up.

With the station now becoming a raging inferno, they could no longer go through the entrance. "We'll have to go out the back window." Alex headed for the opening that faced the valley below.

Their only plan of escape was at the edge of the mountain with no way down.

FIFTEEN

Rachel looked below them at the sheer drop that was now their only escape.

"I'll lower you down first," Alex told her. "Then Liam. Then this guy. Once you're on the ground, head right." Alex's love for her was shining in his eyes. She smiled up at him, trying her best to reassure him and herself that everything would work out, in spite of what her gut was screaming.

She tucked her weapon behind her back and climbed through the opening, trusting Alex with her life. He grabbed hold of her arms and slowly lowered her down. There was still a three-foot jump. With her heartbeat threatening to drown out all other sound, she nodded and Alex let go. She dropped to the ground and stumbled on the uneven footing. Somehow she managed to catch herself before she slid over the edge and plunged to her death.

Rachel blew out a huge sigh and stood on unsteady legs. Alex was as pale as a sheet, clearly terrified by what he'd just witnessed. "I'm okay," she quickly reassured him.

Liam's descent wasn't nearly as easy. He landed on his injured side, the pain causing him to scream. Rachel rushed to his aid and helped him rise to his feet. They carefully made their way to the safe area. She lowered Liam against a nearby tree and went to help Alex.

The building appeared close to collapsing. "Hurry, Alex, the station won't last much longer!" she called out. Once the captured man dropped down, Rachel kept her weapon pointed at him as he headed over to Liam. Behind her she could hear parts of the station collapsing upon itself.

Alex!

"Keep an eye on him, Liam." Rachel didn't wait for his answer. She had to get to Alex. She couldn't lose him again.

"Alex!" she called out. She couldn't see anything but fire and smoke coming from the rapidly disintegrating station.

Please, be okay.

"Alex!" She screamed in panic. She watched in horror as the station crumbled to the ground. The heat from the blaze so intense that she was forced to look away. Was he inside? Had she lost him? The pain that thought brought shot through her, leaving a path of destruction like a bullet's wound.

The smallest of sounds close by had her whirling around. *Alex!* Singed and bloody, he emerged from the firestorm raging behind him. She ran to him. "You're hurt."

He winced as she held him close. "Just a few cuts and scrapes is all. I barely managed to jump out the window before the place went down. Let's hurry. We can use the fire and smoke as a distraction to get away."

They went back to where Liam had managed to stand and was keeping a close eye on his prisoner.

"Can you walk?" Rachel asked. She could see he was in a lot of pain.

Liam nodded. "I'll keep up. Let's get out of here while we still have a chance."

Rachel motioned to their prisoner to start walking. "You go first."

He tossed her an evil look. "You'll never get away. He has people everywhere up here."

"Just start walking." She wasn't letting him get in her head.

The man headed in the direction she indicated. Liam moved close so that only Rachel and Alex could hear. "He's right. They have dozens of men out here."

Alex nodded. "How did you get turned onto these guys, anyway?"

"Through Deacon." Liam confirmed what they'd suspected. "He's been deep undercover with someone close to Temple's crew for a while. That's how we crossed paths. Temple is the one I've been tracking for a while."

Rachel started to ask her brother where the sarin was hidden. Before she got the question out, they were ambushed by gunfire.

"Take cover," she yelled, and they ducked behind a small grove of trees barely wide enough to cover them. Their prisoner went running in the direction of the shots while yelling for his buddies not to shoot him.

Rachel peered around the tree. A round of gunshots sounded a little ways from them. Someone screamed. She had no idea what was happening. She turned to Liam. He was slumped against the tree next to her. "Liam!" She could see that he'd reopened his wound and was losing blood again.

Alex hurried to help her. "Liam, are you able to walk?"

Rachel shook her head. "He can't go anywhere, Alex."

Liam flinched in pain as she did her best to secure the wound once more.

"No, it's okay, Rachel. I can keep up. We have to get out of here. We'll be trapped if we stick around." Liam words slurred. He barely had the strength to get them out.

Before she could answer, a noise close by sent her whirling toward it. One of the men from earlier had his gun pointed straight at them and was ready to fire. Before she could draw her weapon, a shot rang out. The man's startled expression was the last thing she saw before he dropped to the ground dead.

Rachel searched in the direction from where the shot had come and saw Michelle standing there with a gun in her hand. Before Rachel could fully comprehend what had happened, Michelle dropped her weapon on the ground.

"I can't believe she did that," Rachel murmured to Alex and then said, "Get your hands in the air."

Michelle obeyed and Alex grabbed her weapon. "You saved our lives," Alex said in amazement. "Why would you do that?"

But Rachel believed she knew. "You're the asset who is working with Deacon, aren't you?" Michelle managed a frightened nod. "You did the right thing. You're better off with us. Temple will kill you if he discovers you helped us out."

* * *

"Where are the others?" Alex asked, wondering how she'd managed to get away from Temple and his men.

"The two that were here are dead. I shot them. Your prisoner got away. The rest of Temple's crew will have heard the shots. They'll be here soon. We need to get out of here before that happens."

"How do you fit into all this, Michelle?" Rachel asked. She appeared just as confused by what happened as he was. "You had your chance to get away before and you didn't take it. Why help us now?"

"I couldn't before. I didn't trust you...and I was scared of him. He threatened me. But I can't let him go through with what he has planned. It's too horrible."

Rachel's gaze collided with Alex's. "Who are you talking about?"

"Peter... Blake Temple," she amended. "He's not who he says he is. He's a monster. Please, you have to stop him."

"What's he planning with the sarin gas?" Alex asked.

"How did you know about that?" Michelle looked at Alex in surprise.

"Let's just say we put two and two together.

We know Temple and the rest of his men faked their deaths," added Rachel.

Michelle looked from one to the other. "Who are you people?"

Alex wondered how much they could trust her. But she had saved their lives. "I'm CIA, just like Deacon. You can trust us."

Michelle appeared unconvinced. "You'll understand if I don't. Temple said he was CIA, too, and he did terrible things. He forced me to work for him."

Before she could say anything more, another round of shots rang out close by.

"Duck," Alex yelled, and they slipped back behind their tree coverage.

"That's him." Michelle's eyes grew wide with fear. "He'll kill me. He'll kill all of us."

"We're not going to let that happen," Alex assured her.

Before Michelle could respond, the woods around them detonated with gunfire.

Rachel glanced over at him. "We can't hold them off much longer."

Alex searched their surrounding woods. "We'll have to make a run for it. Liam, can you make it?"

Liam was barely hanging on, but he was quick to assure him. "I can." Alex slid a look

Rachel's way. He could read all of her skepticism, yet they were out of options.

He pointed deeper into the wilderness behind them. "That's our only way. Go, Rachel."

Rachel grabbed Liam around the waist and took off running with Michelle following. Alex covered them as best he could until he was certain they were safe, then he left his hiding spot and ran as fast as possible while shots flew past him, barely missing him several times.

Alex caught up with them. "We bought ourselves some time. I just hope Jase and the team get here soon. We can't hold Temple's men off for long."

As they hurried through the woods, Alex kept a careful eye behind them. So far, no one was following. His gut told him it was only a matter of time before that changed.

SIXTEEN

It felt like the nightmare would never end. Rachel could hear the men tramping through the woods at a fast click.

Alex glanced over his shoulder. "I see them. We are way outnumbered."

With her heart threatening to explode against her chest, Rachel could feel each breath as it burned her lungs.

She was barely hanging on. She couldn't imagine how difficult the trek had been for Liam. He looked as if he was ready to drop. Her brother stumbled and almost took her with him. "Alex, we have to find a place to hide. Liam can't take much more."

She glanced around, searching for anyplace where they might take cover to wait it out until the Scorpion team arrived.

"Over there." She spotted a thick grove of trees off to the right where it was impossible to see inside. "It's worth a try."

The four of them headed for the grove. If their plan worked, Temple's men would keep going straight.

As they entered the wooded area, Rachel could barely see a few inches in front of her.

With Alex's help, she slowly eased Liam down to the ground. She could see he was close to losing consciousness again. *Please let help arrive soon.*

Next to her Rachel could feel Michelle trembling. If Temple and his men realized she had been helping Deacon all along, they would kill her without asking questions.

Over the drumming of her heartbeat, Rachel heard the men working their way through the woods. They were almost right on top of them now.

Michelle came close to screaming. Rachel covered her mouth with her hand. They couldn't afford to be found out.

"Do you see them? They were just here." McNamara sounded as if he'd been running a marathon.

"No, but they can't be far. They have Carlson with them and he's injured. That should slow them down," answered a man she didn't recognize.

Silence followed while Rachel held on to a breath.

"Temple wants them found now. Who knows who they've contacted? We're running out of time and our buyer is waiting. If we don't deliver the sarin soon, it will be bad for us. These people don't accept excuses," McNamara said.

Rachel reached for Alex's hand and held it tight. As an answered prayer, she heard the men slowly move away from the spot.

"I think they're gone," Alex whispered. "We need to get back to the station, where Jase is expecting us to be."

Rachel looked down at Liam. He hadn't regained consciousness. Tears filled her eyes. They couldn't leave him here.

"I've got him." Alex hauled Liam up beside him. It was going to take all of his strength to get Liam back to the station, yet he never hesitated. "You and Michelle head out. I'll be right behind you."

She shook her head. "I'll follow you. In case those men circle back. Otherwise, you'll be vulnerable."

He slowly agreed. It was their only option. "Okay. Michelle, you know the way. Don't try anything foolish."

The woman was clearly terrified of McNamara. Rachel didn't doubt for a moment that Michelle had suffered terrible things at Temple's and McNamara's hands.

With Alex all but hauling Liam beside him, it was slow going. It felt as if it took forever for them to make any time at all.

Rachel kept a close eye behind them. She was afraid the noise they were making would attract the men's attention. So far, they seemed to have bought their decoy. But for how long?

Several times, Alex had to stop to catch his breath. Michelle kept a careful watch out for them. Whenever they stopped, she did, as well. As much as Rachel wanted to trust her, she couldn't bring herself to fully. She'd worked for Temple. To what degree she had been involved in his organization was still undetermined.

Rachel eased up next to Alex and put her arms around Liam, too. "Let me help you. We can make better time together."

He nodded and they slowly made their way along the path. They were still some distance from the station, but she could see it burning above the treetops.

Behind them, Rachel heard something. She stopped, as did Alex. "That has to be them. We need to hurry."

They did everything they could to go faster, but it was impossible. They stumbled several times and almost fell.

"We'll never outrun them. We have to find a place to take cover," she told Alex.

He shook his head. "We're almost there."

Rachel grabbed hold of Liam again and she and Alex all but ran with his dead weight between them.

"I see them. They're up ahead," McNamara yelled. "Don't let them get away."

"We have to hurry, Rachel," Alex urged.

She felt as if she were running blindly, not sure how much farther she could go.

Michelle grabbed the weapon Rachel had tucked behind her back. "Go. Let me cover you. I can slow them down for a bit to buy you some time."

Rachel glanced at Alex. "It's our only chance."

Alex slowly nodded and they took off running again.

Behind them, shots ricocheted through the woods.

Once they reached the destroyed station, they found a safe place to hide.

"I don't hear anything." Rachel listened over the noise of her pulse and the fire raging, but there was only silence.

"I don't, either. I hope she got out of there safe. Stay here with Liam. I'm going after her."

Rachel clutched his hand. "Be careful, please."

He smiled down at her and squeezed her

hand before heading back to where they had left Michelle.

Rachel glanced over at Liam. Her brother was mumbling incoherently.

Lord, we need Your help…

She barely got the words out when she heard multiple shots fired. *Alex!*

Seconds later, more than one set of footsteps came their way. Rachel got to her feet and drew her weapon. She wasn't going down without a fight.

With the rifle ready to fire, Alex charged into the wooded area with Michelle close behind.

He spotted the weapon and stopped dead in his tracks. "Whoa. Hang on, there, Rachel. It's just us."

She slowly lowered the weapon. Relief threatened to buckle her knees. She was on edge. They all were. They needed the nightmare to end soon.

"They're almost here." *Where are you, Jase?* He didn't want to show Rachel how worried he was, but they couldn't hold out much longer. McNamara and his men were almost right on top of them and Liam was fading fast. If they didn't get help soon, none of them would be walking out of here alive.

"We know you're in there." McNamara

stopped in front of their hiding spot. "Come out with your hands up and we might let you live. If we have to come get you, it'll be a different story."

Rachel was close enough to see all of Alex's uncertainties. He didn't know what to do. Should they keep fighting? Or give up? If they did, would McNamara let them live long enough for Jase to reach them?

McNamara ordered his men to fire on them. Shots riddled through the space where they stood, forcing them down to the ground.

Their time was now measured in minutes. Rachel took his hand and looked into his eyes. Seconds passed while he just took in her beauty. Was this the end for them?

She leaned over and kissed him tenderly. "It will be okay. We just have to keep believing."

He nodded. He so wanted to believe that, but desperation made it difficult to hold on to his faith. He loved her. He didn't want to die without letting her know how much.

Alex cupped her face. There were tears in her eyes. She understood what possibly lay ahead for them, as well. "I love you, Rachel. I love you so much."

A sob escaped and she hugged him tight. "I love you, too, Alex."

"Last chance. Surrender or die." McNamara's ultimatum interrupted the intimate moment.

Alex brushed a tear from her cheek. "I know that, and I never stopped loving you, either. I'm just so sorry I messed things up between us before. I should have listened to what you needed. I should have been there for you."

She shook her head. "No, you were right. I had no business putting demands on you. Just because I was ready to leave the CIA didn't mean you were, too. I should have listened to what you wanted. I shouldn't have run away from you."

He tugged her closer. "None of that matters now. We love each other. That's all that matters. I love you so much and with God's help, we will get through this."

She smiled up at him. She had enough faith for the both of them and he was grateful. "You're right. We will."

But they both knew there was only one option left for them. Giving themselves up was their only chance, but convincing Michelle of this would not be so easy. Alex told her what they must do.

Her reaction wasn't a surprise. "I can't. He'll kill me." Alex didn't doubt for a second that her fears were justified.

"You're right, he will. You should head out,"

he told Michelle. "We'll turn ourselves in. They still need us to find the sarin. Take the gun. My team should be here soon."

Michelle was stunned that Alex would let her go. "Thank you for trusting me," she said with heartfelt gratitude. "I don't know how to repay you."

"You saved our lives," Rachel said. "You don't need to repay us. But you need to hurry. We can't hold them off much longer."

As Michelle went deeper into the wilderness thicket behind them, Alex prayed he hadn't made a terrible mistake by letting a person go who was at the very least an accomplice to Temple's crimes.

When he was satisfied she was a safe distance away, he looked down at Rachel. "Are you ready for this?"

She didn't hesitate. "Yes. I'm ready. We'll get through this, Alex. I know we will." Her strength reminded him of all the times they'd fought side by side.

Alex let her go and they got to their feet. "McNamara, we're coming out. Hold your fire. I want your word you're not going to shoot us. Otherwise, you'll never find the sarin."

A tense silence followed. Alex wondered if McNamara and the rest of Temple's goons had already located the sarin. If so, they wouldn't hesitate to kill all of them.

"All right, you have my word. Put your weapons down and come out with your hands up."

Alex blew out a sigh. They hadn't found the gas yet.

Rachel didn't seem at all convinced. "Do you believe him?"

He didn't, but he didn't want her to give up. "I do. He has no idea where the sarin is. They need us. Follow my lead, okay?"

She slowly nodded. "Let's do this."

Alex lowered his weapon to the ground and Rachel followed his lead. With one final look into her beautiful eyes, and a prayer for safety chasing through his head, he took Rachel's hand and stepped out of the coverage to face five armed men.

McNamara stared at them through narrowed eyes. "Where are the others?"

"Carlson's injured. He's in there. Your friend Michelle got away."

McNamara stepped inches from Alex's face. "You're lying. She's working with you. I saw her helping you."

Alex shook his head. "I don't know what you saw, but she tried to shoot us."

McNamara motioned to one of his flunkies. "Check it out."

The man clearly wasn't thrilled to be heading into what could be a bloodbath, but he knew better than to disobey McNamara's command. He eased through the opening. He wasn't in there long before he returned. "Carlson's in there. He's unconscious. He won't be telling us anything. *She's* gone."

"You expect me to believe Michelle overpowered both of you and got away?" McNamara asked. When they didn't answer he said, "It doesn't matter, she won't get far. I'll take care of her soon enough."

Alex wasn't going to let McNamara hurt Michelle. They'd need her to help them fit the pieces of Temple's crimes together and put them away for the rest of their lives.

"So with your friend in there unable to help us find our product, why should we keep you two alive? You've been useless so far."

"Because Carlson told me where he hid the gas. If you want your product, you'd better hope we both stay unharmed," Alex told him.

McNamara didn't believe him, but he was all out of options. "All right. Let's say you know where it's hidden. Tell me where, and I'll have my men check it out. If you're telling the truth, I'll let you both live."

Alex's thoughts churned like crazy trying to

come up with a believable location. There was only one that came to mind. "It's at the lodge."

McNamara grinned his disbelief. "Nice try, but we've already been there, remember? There's nothing there but a decaying old building."

Alex kept his expression blank. "That's because you didn't look in the right place."

McNamara's interest was piqued as he tried to determine if he was telling the truth. "And where might the right place be?"

Alex could think of only one option the man might buy. "Under the floorboards in the great room. Carlson told me he hid it there."

McNamara looked as if he hadn't heard him correctly. "The floorboards," he said doubtfully. "You're lying. There's nothing there."

"Am I? Do you want the sarin or not?"

Wavering, McNamara grabbed his cell phone and tried it, then raged at the lack of service— the fire must have destroyed the phone lines. He turned to two of his men. "Head back that way. Tell Blake where the sarin is supposed to be." He tossed Alex a threatening glance. "Let me know if it's not there as soon as possible."

The two men headed back in the direction of the lodge. McNamara came over to where Alex stood. Taking the butt of his gun, he slammed it into Alex's midsection. Alex doubled over in pain as air evaporated from his lungs. It took forever for him to be able to breathe normally again.

"That's for all the trouble you two have caused us so far," McNamara growled heartlessly. Alex slowly straightened, trying not to show any reaction.

"You'd better hope for your sake and hers that you're telling the truth. Otherwise, your deaths will be slow, and you, little sister, can watch your brother die a very painful death."

SEVENTEEN

Rachel put her arm around Alex's waist to help him stand. McNamara saw it and yanked her away, dragging her over to one of his men. "Keep an eye on her." To the other man he barked, "Get Carlson out here. I don't trust him out of my sight."

The man rushed to do McNamara's bidding while Rachel's mind went crazy with worry. Liam was so weak. He could have internal injuries they didn't know about. He needed to be kept as still as possible.

The man returned, dragging Liam in his arms. He dumped him on the ground at McNamara's feet.

Rachel broke free of her captor and knelt close to her brother. She cradled Liam's head in her lap.

"Leave him alone. He can't help you with anything." She stared up at McNamara in defiance.

"Then your friend had better be telling the truth. Otherwise, I'll force you to watch him die."

It took everything inside of her to hold it together. She was terrified Liam would die up here on the mountain and there was nothing they could do to help him or Deacon.

McNamara took out his phone again. "Keep an eye on them. I'm going to try to get a service spot. I need to talk to Blake right away."

Rachel watched as McNamara walked a little ways from them. She glanced over at Alex. This was their only chance. She could see he understood.

She motioned to the man standing near her. Alex gave a tiny nod. She silently counted off three and then jumped to her feet. Before the man knew what she had planned, she struck him hard in the stomach with her fist. He bent over in pain and she grabbed his weapon easily enough.

Once she'd gained the upper hand, she turned. The man guarding Alex charged for her, but Alex grabbed his weapon and he froze.

The man she'd disarmed yelled at the top of his voice. Right away, McNamara jerked around. Seeing what was happening, he came rushing back to the site.

Alex grabbed the man closest to him and

pointed the gun at his head. "That's far enough. Unless you want your friend to die."

McNamara stopped dead in his tracks, hesitating. Then he grinned. "You think I care about him?" Before they knew what he had planned, he shot the man through his chest. Alex just had time to jump sideways before the bullet struck him, as well. The man fell to the ground dead.

Alex fired one shot, striking McNamara in the upper arm near his shoulder. McNamara's weapon flew from his hand. He grabbed his wounded shoulder, screaming in pain.

"You shot me," he raged as if he couldn't believe what was happening. Alex grabbed the weapon he'd lost.

"Don't you dare try anything." Rachel kept her weapon trained on the one remaining man. The man slowly nodded.

Rachel moved to Alex's side. "We need to get out of here before Temple's men realize we were bluffing about the sarin gas."

"We can't leave Liam here. They'll kill him," Alex said.

Rachel turned to the remaining man. "You, get him up."

"I'll help." Alex grabbed Liam's legs and the man took hold of his arms.

Rachel motioned to McNamara. "Get moving."

Before they'd managed but a few steps, Michelle appeared out of the woods.

She pointed her gun straight at McNamara. "You, you deserve to die." All of her anger and hurt was written on her face.

Rachel couldn't let Michelle kill McNamara. They needed him and she would have to live with what she'd done for the rest of her life. "Drop the weapon, Michelle." She zeroed the gun in on the woman. "If you kill him, you'll be just as guilty as he is."

"He and his buddies murdered my husband," she said with tears in her eyes.

Rachel couldn't believe it. "What are you talking about?"

"Shut your mouth," McNamara raged.

"My husband was Robert Ludwick. You know him as the Chemist. He created the recipe for the sarin gas Temple used. Temple and his men promised to pay him for the recipe and his client list. Instead, they killed him and forced me to work for them."

Now it made sense why Michelle had helped them.

"This one, he shot my husband in front of me." She waved the gun at McNamara. "He deserves to die."

Rachel took a step closer. "You're right, he deserves to pay for what he did to your husband, but don't let him destroy you in the process. He's not worth it. You still have a chance at a life, Michelle. Don't throw that away for him. It's too precious."

Tears spilled from Michelle's eyes and she sobbed, her heart breaking. Slowly, she lowered the weapon.

Rachel went over and put her arm around her. "It's going to be okay. We'll make sure they all pay for what they've done...thanks to you."

Michelle finally managed a smile as she brushed away her tears. "Promise me?"

Rachel gladly gave that promise.

"Ladies, we need to get out of here now. We don't know where the rest of Temple's goons are." Alex motioned to McNamara to get moving.

With Michelle guarding McNamara, the man in front of Alex took hold of Liam once more.

As they headed through the woods at a slow pace, Rachel kept a close eye behind them to make sure no one was coming after them. Thanks to God, they now had breathing room.

"I'm sorry about your husband," she told Michelle. "I lost mine, too."

Michelle looked at her in shock. "You did? I'm so sorry. I know how difficult it is, losing someone you love."

It had been. She'd loved Brian so much and

she was grateful for the time they had together. But part of her heart had always belonged to Alex. He'd been her first love. They'd shared so much together. Like it or not, their pasts were forever linked to each other.

Rachel so wanted to live long enough to find out what the future held for them. Yet she couldn't shake the feeling that Alex was a career agent. It was his calling and he was good at it. She couldn't ask him to leave again and she couldn't live that type of life. She was done with the shadow games. She needed to live in the light. Would he surprise her and walk away from the CIA? Or would he break her heart again when he left for the next mission? She didn't think she could bear going through that much pain again, but somehow she would manage for him. Because she wouldn't keep him from doing what he needed to do.

A noise in the distance captured his attention. It sounded like…choppers. More than one! Jase was here.

Rachel heard it, as well. "Is that…?"

His smile broadened. "It's my team. Rachel, it's almost over." He lowered Liam's legs to the ground. The man did the same. "Keep an eye on the both of them for me, Michelle."

"It will be my pleasure." Michelle moved

closer to McNamara while keeping the second man in her sights. Alex glanced over at the raging inferno that had once been the ranger station. "They won't have any way to know we're still here. We have to find a way to get their attention." He remembered the flare gun he'd taken from the station before it collapsed around him. He pulled it out of his pocket. "The station was equipped with this. Once they get closer, we can shoot it off to let them know we're still down here."

Rachel hugged him close and he was so thankful that he'd thought ahead enough to grab the flare gun.

Alex spotted the two Scorpion choppers rising over the mountain edge. He'd been through some terrifying moments while on a mission, yet never had there been a more welcome sight in his opinion. The first chopper hovered above the burning remains while the second one hung back.

Alex aimed the flare gun away from the fire and shot the flare into the air.

The first chopper moved away from the fire and lingered near where they'd seen the flare. Alex left the cover of the trees and began waving frantically. Rachel followed him and did the same.

He could see his friend Aaron Foster at the

helm of the chopper. Aaron banked to the left, looking for a place to land.

"They've seen us. They're landing." He hugged Rachel close once more. He was so happy. They'd survived the nightmare. They weren't alone anymore.

Aaron found a landing spot and brought the chopper slowly to the ground; the dust debris it kicked up had them shielding their eyes against the blast.

Once the first chopper was on the ground, the second found a landing spot a little ways down the mountainside.

With Rachel tucked against his side, Alex hurried toward Aaron's chopper. The door slid open and his good friend Jase Bradford hopped out, followed by several other members of the team.

Jase glanced at the towering inferno. "What happened here?"

Alex gave him a quick rundown. "I have an injured man over here who needs immediate medical attention." He pointed toward Liam. Then he explained about McNamara's injury and where he was located.

Jase motioned to Ryan, the EMT of the group. Along with Gavin, they hurried to assist Liam and bring out McNamara.

"We need to get to Deacon, too. He's in bad

shape and he's been down there alone for a while." Rachel told Jase where the agent was located.

"I'll send Ryan and Aaron down to get him. They can take him and your brother along with McNamara to the hospital right away. I have the state troopers on their way up the mountain as we speak. We'll have this location saturated in no time. Temple and his men won't get away this time."

Alex watched as Ryan and Gavin carefully carried Liam over to the chopper, with McNamara trailing behind them. Liam was strong and Alex believed God would bring him through safely. McNamara appeared defeated. He had to know what lay ahead for him. If he talked, it might help him in the long run.

"Take some of the team with you." Jase gave Aaron the location where Deacon was hiding. "We don't know what you'll find there. Temple's men might have found Deacon by now, so be prepared." Alex prayed Deacon was still alive.

The chopper carrying Liam and McNamara quickly became airborne. Jase waited until it was heading down the mountain before he turned to Rachel and held out his hand.

"Jase Bradford. It's nice to meet you." Jase smiled.

Rachel shook his hand. She seemed to be unable to grasp that they'd finally been rescued. She had a surreal look on her face. "Rachel Simmons. I can't tell you how happy we are to see you."

Jase laughed. "I can imagine it's been a crazy few hours up here."

Michelle emerged from her hiding place with her prisoner in front of her.

With everything that had happened, Rachel had forgotten about Michelle guarding another of McNamara's men. Alex explained what he knew about Michelle's role in everything along with what she'd done to help them.

Agent Liz Ramirez took the weapon from Michelle and then cuffed her prisoner.

"I appreciate you helping my people, but you have to understand, you're still a suspect in all of this until we know what truly took place." Jase indicated Liz should put Michelle and the man into the remaining chopper. "Keep an eye on both of them."

Michelle's story would get sorted out in time. She'd be treated fairly.

"We found agent Seth Jamison's body a little ways down from here." Alex filled Jase in on what he believed happened to Liam's handler.

"Unbelievable. I guess that's how Temple and his men managed to stay hidden for so long. They had inside assistance." Jase shook his head.

They'd sort through the web of lies in time. Right now, Alex's main concern was locating Temple and his men before they found the sarin gas. "We need to go after Temple's people before they get away. Or worse, locate the gas."

Jase nodded. "You're right." He motioned to the rest of the team standing by. "Fan out. Keep your eyes open. They have lots of men up here and they have nothing to lose."

Jase turned to him and Rachel. "You two should hang back. You both look exhausted. We've got this."

Standing next to him, Alex could feel Rachel ready to protest. He was right there with her. They'd come this far. "No way. We want to see this through to the end."

Jase didn't appear surprised. "All right, but be careful."

The airborne chopper was still in sight when it opened fire on something down below.

Alex focused on the area. "It looks like they've located some of Temple's men." The team rushed for the location. Alex stuck close to Rachel. They were both drop-dead exhausted, but they'd come this far. They weren't about to give up the fight without knowing its ending.

The chopper hovered over an area, occasionally firing. Alex heard the men return shots, then silence followed.

Rachel glanced at Alex. "What happened?"

He shook his head. "I don't know. I'm guessing they realized they were outnumbered and gave up."

Once the team reached the site, the chopper took off again. There were half a dozen men standing with their hands in the air. Within no time, they were subdued in cuffs.

As Alex looked over the faces of the men who had surrendered, he realized none of them were Temple's CIA team. They'd somehow managed to get away.

Jase came over to where they stood and confirmed the truth. "Temple and the rest of the agents aren't here."

Alex couldn't believe they'd gotten away. "Let's just hope he hasn't located the gas already." Alex told Jase what they overheard Mc-Namara say about the prospective buyer.

"That doesn't sound good. We need to find these guys and soon." Jase glanced up at the threatening skies. "It's getting colder and we're running out of daylight. If we haven't found them by night, they could manage to give us the slip."

Jase ordered some of his team to watch the prisoners. "Let's keep looking," he told the rest. "We're losing daylight fast."

In a matter of hours, the entire mountainside

was crawling with state troopers and agents. Alex didn't believe Temple's team would risk leaving the area. "They're hiding out somewhere. Probably hoping we'll think they've left the mountain."

Rachel stopped walking. "The cave. It's the perfect spot to stay hidden and Temple knows about it. There are several passages, and if they stumble upon the one that we did, they could escape."

"You're right." Alex told Jase about the cave. "I sure hope we find them before they reach the sarin. We have no idea who their buyer is, but we need to put him out of business before he can do any harm." Alex didn't want to think about the possibility of the gas falling into deadly hands. He'd seen enough damage over the past few years by terrorists wanting to promote their own agendas.

They'd lost one of their teammates because he'd gotten tied up with some very bad people. The last thing Alex wanted was more bloodshed. He'd seen enough of that to last him a lifetime. And it was why he'd come to a conclusion while up here. This was it for him. He'd gotten a second chance with Rachel and he wanted a fresh start in life with her. He was ready to come back home to the tiny town of Midnight Mountain and start living a normal life again.

EIGHTEEN

As they approached the cave, Rachel couldn't help but feel as if everything they'd gone through so far would come down to just this moment.

She touched Alex's arm. She was so afraid something bad was going to happen to take away their chance at happiness.

He looked deep in her eyes and she saw the same fears in his. But he did his best to reassure her. "It's going to be okay."

She tried to smile. She so wanted to believe it.

"Jase, we need someone around at the back exit in case they stumble on it. We don't want them to get away. Too much is at stake," Alex told his commander.

Jase agreed, "You're right. Go. You two know where it is. Take some men with you."

Alex pointed to three of the team members.

His fellow patriots. They followed Rachel and Alex as they headed toward the back entrance.

Rachel's thoughts went to Liam. He'd looked so pale when they'd taken him away. She couldn't bear it if anything happened to her brother.

Alex clasped her hand briefly. Their eyes met. His feelings for her were right there for her to see and she wanted to cry. She couldn't think of a single thing to say. Would Temple and his band of corrupt CIA agents win in spite of everything they'd fought so hard to accomplish?

"We'll get them." She glanced up at Alex. He was trying to be strong for her. She needed to be for him, as well.

"You're right. We will."

Rachel located the back entrance of the cave and pointed it out. "Over there."

They eased closer. If Temple's team was in there, she didn't believe they'd had enough time to find the escape route yet. But there were dozens of other passages throughout the cave. There could be another way out. She and Alex knew the cave better than anyone and even they hadn't known about the exit.

She turned back to the three men. "Stay here. Alex and I will check it out."

The three agents looked to Alex, who nodded. Then he and Rachel headed inside.

As hard as she tried, Rachel couldn't shake the feeling that something bad was about to happen. Alex must have sensed her struggle.

He drew her close and whispered against her ear. "It's almost over."

As they headed down the same narrow passage they'd taken before, her heart was hammering in her chest. She so wanted to have another chance at a future…with Alex.

Alex stopped and grabbed her arm. She heard it, too. Voices.

"They're CIA and she's with them. It's over, Blake. We should just turn ourselves in and face the music," said a voice she didn't recognize.

The only answer was a single gunshot. Then the sound of something dropping to the ground. She didn't doubt for a second that Temple had killed the man. Trapped like animals, they were turning on each other. Would they kill themselves before Alex's team had the chance to interrogate them?

She mouthed, "We need them alive."

She and Alex charged Temple's men. She didn't doubt that the three men standing guard outside would have heard the shot and would follow.

Surprised, the men whirled with weapons

drawn. One man lay on the ground at Temple's feet.

They stood facing each other in a silent stand-off.

"Drop your weapons. Otherwise, you're not getting out of here alive," Alex ordered.

Rachel counted the remaining men. Three. There was something wrong. One of the team was missing. Had he escaped a different way or…?

Before she'd finished the thought, someone grabbed her from behind. A gun was shoved against her temple.

"Drop your weapon unless you want her to die," the man behind her yelled.

Rachel's gaze locked with Alex. She was so afraid. She didn't want to die. Not like this.

"Take it easy." Alex tried to keep the man calm. "You don't want to do that. There are dozens of agents all around. None of you are walking out of here free."

"Shoot her. I've got him," Temple ordered the man.

"I said drop your gun." Her captor's hand shook nervously on the weapon. Rachel knew if she did as he asked, she'd be at the man's mercy. That would leave Alex alone. She couldn't do it.

Alex's gaze sliced to the side. He was trying

to tell her something. The three Scorpion team members were close.

She managed the tiniest of nods.

"Okay, stay calm. I'm lowering my weapon now." She held the gun out in front of her. With the man still clutching her, she managed to slowly ease the weapon down to the ground.

"Now," Alex yelled. Rachel jabbed her foot hard into the captor's shin. He let her go and she hit the ground. Alex fired; the shot hit the man in his arm. The weapon flew from his hand. Rachel fired at Temple before he could get a shot off, striking him in the upper torso.

Before the remaining men could manage even a single shot, the three Scorpion agents appeared with weapons drawn.

"Shoot them," Temple raged while rolling around in pain. "You can take them. We can still get out of this."

"Don't do it," Rachel warned. "You still have a chance to live. You don't have to die here."

As the standoff continued, the men seemed to be debating on whether or not they stood a chance at surviving. Behind them, Jase and the rest of his team reached them.

Realizing they were severely outnumbered, Temple's men slowly lowered their weapons.

"Get a medical chopper up here right away. We have injured men," Jase told one of his guys.

But Rachel was no longer listening. She ran to Alex and threw her arms around him. She was so grateful that they'd made it through alive.

He held her close for the longest time. Then he framed her face and kissed her tenderly.

She loved him so much. She didn't want to deny it any longer. She loved him and she was so afraid he would choose the job over her once more.

"Temple shot his own guy dead," Alex told his friend. "He wanted to surrender. Temple wasn't going down without a fight."

Jase came over to where they stood. "We need to get these two to a hospital. The rest of the men will be taken into custody. We'll interview them separately. Let's see if we can get one of them to talk about who was supposed to buy the sarin gas."

Rachel still couldn't believe how close to dying she'd come. "Is there any news on my brother?" She had to know Liam was okay.

Jase's smile broadened. "The cell service up here is horrible, but I just got the word. He's going to be fine. He'll be in the hospital for a while, though. Deacon's touch and go. He was in pretty bad shape when Ryan reached him."

She said a silent prayer for Deacon's recovery. He'd fought so hard to live even though his injuries had been severe. Deacon had tried to help Michelle get away from Temple. He'd done his best to bring down Temple and his thugs. He didn't deserve to die because of his loyalty.

"I know where the gas is hidden." Alex glanced down at Rachel as he spoke.

Jase stared at him in surprise. "Where?"

"The cave Liam mentioned in his letter," Alex said to Rachel. "He was trying to tell me without saying it directly in case the letter fell into the wrong hands. Liam must have realized that Seth was dirty and was fearful he'd find the letter somehow."

"We need to find the sarin as soon as possible," Jase said. "And we need to find the rest of Temple's men. I have the state troopers combing the woods. There were some at the lodge. They'd been digging up the floor. They said they thought the gas was there." Jase shook his head.

"I guess they bought my story after all." Alex told him what had happened before they arrived.

"Unbelievable." Jase gave them both the once-over. Alex couldn't imagine how horrible they must look. "Ryan's on his way back here to take these injured men to the hospital. I want him to take a look at the both of you. You look as if you could use a little medical attention."

Once air emergency services arrived, they

prepared Temple and the other injured man for the trip. Ryan and Aaron were with them.

Exhausted to his core, Alex asked Ryan to take a look at Rachel first. She'd been through so much and she wasn't used to being in the field anymore.

Alex wasn't about to stay behind until he'd found out the ending of the story. Why Liam and Deacon had risked their lives.

He waited until Ryan had finished his exam of Rachel and had treated her cuts and scrapes. "I'm going with them," he told her gently. "I want to know that the sarin is safe. Liam and Deacon deserve as much."

"I'm coming with you, Alex." But he shook his head. "No, you've been through enough. Go be with Liam. I'll find you again."

He could see all the doubts in her eyes and he understood each of them. He'd let her go once. She believed he would choose the job again.

Before he could reassure her, Ryan came over. "It's time to go. We need to get these guys to the hospital as soon as possible."

Alex nodded. "Give us a second." Ryan faded away and when it was just the two of them again, he didn't know what to say.

She leaned over and kissed him gently. "Go. I'll see you soon."

He hated leaving her, knowing that she had

doubts about his love, but he'd see the mission through to the end, because in his mind it was his last.

Once Rachel had left with Ryan, Alex found Jase.

"So where's this cave?" Jase asked.

"I can take you there. It's some distance away. We can reach it by chopper faster."

"Good. Let's get back to the chopper where Liz and her two prisoners are waiting."

Liz was standing outside waiting for them when they arrived.

"Has he given you any problems?" Jase asked.

She shook her head. "Nothing I couldn't handle."

Before long the state troopers arrived and took Michelle and the other man to a location where Jase and his men could interrogate them.

Aaron piloted the chopper to the cave where Liam had indicated. Alex led the way inside. At first glance, the cave appeared empty. Alex's spirits sank. Had he been wrong? Was Liam simply reminiscing?

"I don't get it. I was positive Liam was trying to tell me something. Let's keep looking. Chances are, he wouldn't have hidden it too close to the entrance in case one of Temple's men stumbled across it."

As they went deeper into the cave, it opened

up into a room that was filled almost to capacity with the sarin gas.

"What were Temple and his men planning to do with all this sarin?" Jase asked in amazement.

"I don't know, but whatever it was, it could have had deadly consequences. Thankfully, we found it before it fell into the wrong hands."

"Yes. It'll take a while to safely get this stuff out of here and stored. Do you want to be part of that? You're the one who brought it to our attention. This is big for you," Jase told him.

Alex shook his head. He had found the sarin for his friend's sake. He'd finished the mission. Now all he could think about was Rachel and the future. She needed to know what he'd decided.

"No, if it's all the same to you, I'll let someone else take the glory." He faced Jase. This man was his friend. Jase had been there for Alex when he'd needed to change jobs within the Agency. But it was time. Still, saying the words to his friend was hard.

"Actually, I think this is my last mission with the Scorpions."

Jase clearly hadn't expected this. It took a good minute for him to answer. "Oh, man, are you leaving us or the Agency?"

Alex believed Jase knew the answer already. "Both, actually."

"I'm going to miss you, buddy. Is this because of Rachel?"

Alex had never told anyone about his history with her. Now he wanted to. "Yes. I love her and I blew it with her once. I don't want to do the same thing again."

Jase slowly smiled. "You're going to be missed tremendously. And if you ever change your mind, you have a place with the Scorpions always, but I get it. Finding someone to love you, well, that's a gift from God. You need to hold on to that with all your heart." He turned to Aaron. "Can you take Alex to the hospital?"

Aaron had overheard their conversation. He nodded quietly, regret showing in his eyes. "Sure thing, buddy. But what Jase said about missing you, well, I second that. I'm going to miss your friendship like crazy."

As they made the trip down to the town of Midnight Mountain, Alex felt the weight of the life he'd been living slowly lift away. His heart soared with the decision he'd made. There would be no regrets for him. No going back. This was the change he'd always wanted, even when he didn't think he needed one. He just prayed that she still wanted the same thing. That she wanted him for the rest of her life.

NINETEEN

She'd been sitting next to her brother's bed for a long time. Liam had wakened long enough to know that she was there and so Rachel was at peace. She'd told him they had Temple's men in custody. He'd mumbled something about Deacon and Rachel had done her best to reassure him. In spite of his injuries, he was holding his own. She'd promised to check on Deacon and had. So far, Deacon's condition hadn't changed much. Still, his doctors were optimistic. The next twenty-four hours would tell the tale.

Now, as she watched her brother resting, Rachel couldn't get the sadness to leave her heart. Alex had wanted to finish the mission, just as he had in the past. He'd been driven back then. It appeared as if nothing had changed in spite of the love he said he still had for her. So where did that leave them?

She was still sitting next to her brother when

the man in her troubled thoughts came into the room.

She glanced up at him. She'd never seen him look so serious before. Had something happened?

"Did you find the sarin?" she asked when the silence between them stretched out, filled with unanswered questions.

He came over to where she sat. "We did. Thanks to Liam, the gas is going to a secure location away from danger."

"Are Temple's men talking yet?" She held his gaze.

He shook his head. "I don't know. I left as soon as we found the sarin." She tried to understand the meaning behind those words.

"How's he doing?" Alex asked and looked at Liam.

She leaned forward and touched her brother's hand. "He's going to be fine. He was awake earlier. He was asking about Deacon. It's touch and go." She answered Alex's unasked question.

Alex nodded, his gaze still on Liam. "I can't believe this is finally over." He stopped for a second and then looked down at her. "Rachel, I'm done."

She didn't understand what he meant. Done with her? The Agency? "I don't understand…"

He knelt next to her. "I'm done with the CIA.

I told Jase before I came here. I want out. I want…you."

She got to her feet and moved away, unsure of what she was doing. Rachel had to be certain she'd heard him correctly. Losing him again would destroy her.

"Please don't say that unless you mean it." Her voice came out as little more than a whisper.

He came to her, taking hold of her arms. "I mean it, Rachel. I've never been more serious in my life. I want out. I've seen enough death and terror to last me a lifetime. I'm done. I want to move back home to Midnight Mountain…and I want a second chance with you. I want to love you for the rest of my life."

She'd waited years to hear him say those words. He finally wanted the same thing as she did. She went into his arms and held him close for a moment and then she kissed him and was so grateful that what happened between them in the past hadn't defined their future. They had a second chance.

"It's about time you two got it together." They turned at the sound of Liam's voice. He was awake and grinning at them. "I was afraid you'd blow it again."

Rachel laughed at her brother's typical Liam saying and smiled up at Alex. "We did get it together, thanks to you. You gave us a second chance, Liam." She kissed Alex again. She would be forever grateful that even though they'd gone through one of the darkest moments of their lives up on the mountain, they'd found each other again.

EPILOGUE

"Babe, I'm home." Alex closed the front door against the chilly Wyoming morning and called out to his wife. It was still dark out, yet he knew she was awake.

Almost a year had now passed since he and Rachel had married. They'd settled back into her place and Alex had found his calling as a cattle rancher. This was a childhood dream both he and Liam shared.

"In here." She peeked her head out of the kitchen. Dressed in a robe, her hair tousled from sleep and seven months pregnant, she still took his breath away.

He was so excited about becoming a father. He went to the kitchen and drew her back against him, his hands splaying across her midsection. Their child. He was so happy. There was a time when he couldn't imagine ever being this happy.

"How's the little one today?" he asked and kissed her neck.

She covered his hands with hers. "Active. I think she's ready to come out." He and Rachel teased each other about whether they were having a girl or a boy. She insisted a girl, while he felt obligated to say a boy. Truthfully, he didn't care. He was just so happy to be having a child with her.

That time over a year ago had faded into a memory now. The pain and fear they'd both experienced were all but gone. Liam was safe. Deacon had recovered from his injuries, and thanks to Michelle, they had the buyer for the sarin gas in custody and Temple and his men had gone away for a very long time.

Thanks to God, he and Rachel had made good on the second chance God gave them.

"How's the ranch coming along?" she asked as she put the eggs on to cook.

He loved watching her. She was so beautiful. At times, he still couldn't believe she was his bride.

Since Liam's last mission, he, too, had left the CIA. He and Alex had decided to use the property Brian left Rachel to buy some cattle to run there, as well as keep up the horse ranch.

So far, it had been a learning experience for both him and Liam, but Alex loved it and he found himself looking forward to each new day…with her.

Rachel caught him watching her and immediately ran a hand through her hair. "I must look like a mess."

He shook his head and planted a kiss on her lips. She had no idea how lovely she was to him. "You've never looked prettier." He gathered her close. "I love you, Rachel. I love you so much. I still can't believe I'm blessed enough to have this life with you."

Tears filled her eyes. She cried a lot lately. Hormones. "I'm the blessed one. I thought I'd lost you for good. I'm so glad God brought us together again."

"Me, too," he whispered, and then kissed her gently and held her close. He'd forever be grateful to God for bringing them back into each other's lives. He thought he'd lost this part of his life for good. But God with His infinite perfect timing had chosen the right moment for them, and he'd spend the rest of his life trying to be worthy of this wonderful life he had.

* * * * *

*If you enjoyed this book, don't miss these
other exciting stories from Mary Alford:*

*FORGOTTEN PAST
ROCKY MOUNTAIN PURSUIT
DEADLY MEMORIES
FRAMED FOR MURDER*

Available now from Love Inspired Suspense!

*Find more great reads at
www.LoveInspired.com.*

Dear Reader,

There's just something about first love stories that warm the heart, especially when a love that was believed lost forever is rekindled once again.

For Alex Booth and Rachel Simmons, their high school romance ended bitterly when their jobs with the CIA got in the way. Rachel wanted to have a normal life and family, but Alex couldn't imagine living without the adrenaline rush of the job, and so they parted. Rachel left the CIA for good, and Alex always regretted letting her go.

When Rachel's brother and fellow CIA agent Liam Carlson goes missing in the mountains near Rachel's Wyoming home of Midnight Mountain, there's only one person she trusts enough to ask for help. And that's Alex.

With the two reunited once more, their desperate search to bring Liam home is clouded by old resentments and misunderstanding from the past. Together, Alex and Rachel must find a way to put the past behind them in order to find Liam before the men chasing him finish the job they started and end Liam's life.

Standoff at Midnight Mountain is a story about forgiveness and second chances. I hope

Alex and Rachel's story will touch your heart and bring a smile to your face. And maybe help you remember your own first love.

I so love hearing from readers. Email me at: maryjalfordauthor@gmail.com or write me c/o Love Inspired, 195 Broadway, 24th Floor, New York, NY 10007. Visit me at www.MaryAlford.net and at: https://www.Facebook.com/Mary-AlfordAuthor.

Warmest blessings,
Mary Alford

Get 4 FREE REWARDS!

We'll send you 2 FREE Books plus 2 FREE Mystery Gifts.

Love Inspired® books feature contemporary inspirational romances with Christian characters facing the challenges of life and love.

FREE Value Over **$20**

Get 4 FREE REWARDS!

We'll send you 2 FREE Books plus 2 FREE Mystery Gifts.

Harlequin® Heartwarming™ Larger-Print books feature traditional values of home, family, community and most of all—love.

FREE Value Over **$20**

YES! Please send me 2 FREE Harlequin® Heartwarming™ Larger-Print novels and my 2 FREE mystery gifts (gifts worth about $10 retail). After receiving them, if I don't wish to receive any more books, I can return the shipping statement marked "cancel." If I don't cancel, I will receive 4 brand-new larger-print novels every month and be billed just $5.49 per book in the U.S. or $6.24 per book in Canada. That's a savings of at least 19% off the cover price. It's quite a bargain! Shipping and handling is just 50¢ per book in the U.S. and 75¢ per book in Canada*. I understand that accepting the 2 free books and gifts places me under no obligation to buy anything. I can always return a shipment and cancel at any time. The free books and gifts are mine to keep no matter what I decide.

161/361 IDN GMY3

Name (please print)

Address   Apt. #

City   State/Province   Zip/Postal Code

Mail to the Reader Service:
IN U.S.A.: P.O. Box 1341, Buffalo, NY 14240-8531
IN CANADA: P.O. Box 603, Fort Erie, Ontario L2A 5X3

Want to try two free books from another series? Call 1-800-873-8635 or visit www.ReaderService.com.

---

*Terms and prices subject to change without notice. Prices do not include applicable taxes. Sales tax applicable in N.Y. Canadian residents will be charged applicable taxes. Offer not valid in Quebec. This offer is limited to one order per household. Books received may not be as shown. Not valid for current subscribers to Harlequin Heartwarming Larger-Print books. All orders subject to approval. Credit or debit balances in a customer's account(s) may be offset by any other outstanding balance owed by or to the customer. Please allow 4 to 6 weeks for delivery. Offer available while quantities last.

Your Privacy—The Reader Service is committed to protecting your privacy. Our Privacy Policy is available online at www.ReaderService.com or upon request from the Reader Service. We make a portion of our mailing list available to reputable third parties that offer products we believe may interest you. If you prefer that we not exchange your name with third parties, or if you wish to clarify or modify your communication preferences, please visit us at www.ReaderService.com/consumerchoice or write to us at Reader Service Preference Service, P.O. Box 9062, Buffalo, NY 14240-9062. Include your complete name and address.

HW18

HOME on the RANCH

READERSERVICE.COM

Manage your account online!

- Review your order history
- Manage your payments
- Update your address

*We've designed the
Reader Service website
just for you.*

Enjoy all the features!

- Discover new series available to you,
  and read excerpts from any series.
- Respond to mailings and special
  monthly offers.
- Browse the Bonus Bucks catalog and
  online-only exculsives.
- Share your feedback.

Visit us at:

ReaderService.com